PERILOUS
LOVE
Sinful Souls
MC Book 1

Amo Jones

Perilous Love
Sinful Souls MC Book One

Amo Jones

Formatting by Swish Design & Editing
Editing by Karen's Book Haven
Cover design by Amo Jones
Cover image Bigstock Photo

© 2015 Amo Jones
All rights reserved.

ISBN-13: 978-1517728922
IBSN-10: 1517728924

Note: This story is not suitable for persons under the age of 18 or those who do not enjoy sexy, twisted relationships. This is a roller coaster not a carousel.

*If the word "fuck" offends you, please don't read this book.

Welcome to the twisted world of Alaina Vance and Zane Matthews.

DEDICATION

To all my beautiful mother, thank you for having my back and always believing in me. I love you.

ACKNOWLEDGMENTS

Simon—My partner in crime, the Clyde to my Bonnie, and the love of my life. I could not have done all of this without your undying support. You have been the truth to my words and my number one critic. I love you so much, and I cherish the moments you have had to (at times) take up both roles, as mother and father while I locked myself up in my writing cave. I love you - *always and forever.*

My four little people—My four little critters who are the light of my life. They have tolerated at times a moody mother when all I wanted to do was write, but they enjoy all my guilt gifts and privileges once I'm finished a book, though. So it's a win-win.

Isis Te Tuhi—Thank you for always being the ear to my troubles, for going through the emotional rollercoasters of all these stories with me, you are my caramel soul sister. *The one and only, Mrs. R.F.*

Karen Mandeville-Steer—Oh man, where should I start? Thank you so much for your magic. Thank you for making this book shine and adding color to a once black and white canvas. You are incredible and I will forever be thankful. You are my person.

Kaylene Osborn—You are such an amazing woman, Kay. You have always gone above and beyond with helping me work through my troubles, even if it's not in your job description. I will always value and appreciate all that you do and have done with me. Thank you times a million.

My Readers—My beautiful readers, I love you all. Keep reading and keep writing those reviews. Each of you has contributed to me pushing through my rough patches. You make it all worth it, each and every one of you.

The Bloggers—Thank you to all the lovely bloggers who have been there from day one, and the new ones who have just started reading my stories now and sharing your honest reviews. You are all amazing and I thank you for taking the time out of your busy lives to read my book. I hold the utmost respect for you.

Lastly, thank you to all who have had to endure my yapping as I got excited about a plot in one of my books and all I wanted to do was talk about it. I know I talked your ears off, *so thank you.*

PERILOUS
LOVE *Sinful Souls MC Book 1*

PROLOGUE

ALAINA

New Zealand
Fifteen Years Ago

"Quick Alaina, pack a bag and just put the things you will need in, our flight's leaving in twelve hours and we need to be at the airport in two," my Mom said as she was rushing around our family home.

"Why? Why do we have to leave? I don't understand?" I watched her as she threw clothes in my suitcase.

"You won't understand yet, honey, but one day it will be explained to you. We must go, now."

She was zipping up the bags when I asked, "Where are we going?"

Handing me my bags, she replied, "To stay with your nana and poppa in Westbeach, California. Now please hurry, we don't have long." A sudden loud smash echoed from downstairs. "Alaina, quick!" she said, shoving me towards the window.

My once beautiful mother, who never had a worry in the world, now looked like the devil himself was chasing her.

She pulled open the window. "Aunt Whitney will be outside the gate ready to take us. GO!"

I climbed out the window, looking back to her. "What about you, Mommy?" Something wasn't right.

She looked at me with sadness in her eyes. "Mommy will be right behind you, sweetheart, just go." A knot formed in my throat as I realised she may not be coming. "I love you, Alaina. Always, now leave."

So I did, I climbed down the trellis outside my window and ran. I jumped over our fence, continuing my run until I could see my Aunt's car parked on the curb. Exiting the driver's seat, she took hold of my bag, so I got into the car with her, and waited.

And waited.

But my mom never came.

"We have to leave now, sweetie, I don't think she's coming and I promised your mommy I would take care of you," she assured me, patting my hand.

Tears pooled as confusion set in.

I want my mommy and daddy.

CHAPTER 1

ALAINA

California
Present Day

"You only have one more year of this shit. One more year Alaina, you can do this," I say to myself as I pull a brush through my long blonde hair. It almost never behaves, but today my hair is added to the list of other things going against me. Maybe it will distract from the huge zit on my chin. How those things *magically* pop up out of nowhere, I have no idea.

I scrub my face for what feels like a hundred times, until it is to the point of redness. I pull on my favourite skinny jeans and T-shirt, before heading to my first undergraduate medicine class of the day. School has been difficult at times, but it has always been a dream of mine to become a doctor. Even when I was a little girl, I loved being able to help people.

It's just me and my nana and poppa. They raised me after I left New Zealand. I'd lost count of how many times I'd asked them about my parents and I saw that it was paining them when I'd asked. They had to deal with the uncertainty of their daughter so it wasn't just my grief that I had to consider. The last update we got about five years ago was that the case had gone cold. I had a lot of trouble accepting that and regularly check in with my aunt who answers my calls without a hello, just a 'there's no news, Alaina.'

How can they stop looking for my mom and dad?

They'd revisit it but every avenue ended as a dead end. Poppa asked for everyone's sake to get on with life and don't let the unknowns of our past dictate our future. I still hold out hope that they're alive and my studies have been a good distraction from the merry-go-round of 'what if.' I never told Nana or Poppa that I've been talking to a private investigator who's been doing small checks for me but to do a full scale investigation, the cost is just out of my league. They pushed for me to have an education and make something of myself. I've worked hard and have been working hard to make my grandparents proud of me.

Amo Jones

I'm on my way to my first class, when I get a text from my best friend Vicky. We have known each other since I first moved to Westbeach, when I was eight. She was my first friend and has always stuck up for me. Being from a different country can sometimes be a target for bullies, but she is fiercely loyal.

> Vicky: *I can't believe we have nothing planned to do this weekend...I'm getting an itchy liver, it needs alcohol.*
> Me: *It's Monday. We can plan tonight over tacos. I am worried about that itchy liver...The future doctor in me says that's symptom for primary biliary cirrhosis, but the best friend in me screams too much alcohol!*
> Vicky: *Do not cuss at me, never too much alcohol...You can diagnose me over tequila shots this weekend at The Point. We can start our weekend shenanigans there.*
> Me: *Sounds like a plan :)*

The Point is a bar downtown. It's low key enough to start our night, before we hit the town. It is a little on the rough side, but the drinks are cheap.

I walk into class, pull out the chair at the desk I always sit in and plaster a fake smile on my face. I'm not happy to be back at school at all, and I cannot wait to get home.

The rest of the day goes surprisingly fast and I'm almost back at our dorm when Jesse comes running up behind me. Jesse's been a part of our little circle since we started Westbeach College and I love him like a brother.

"Hey Lain, how was your holiday?" he asks, bouncing a basketball between his legs.

"Oh good, Nana is on her last legs, but she still doesn't fail to make me laugh. How was yours?"

I notice his build has had a lot of attention since the last time I saw him, and his short hair has grown out a little. The girls walking by checking him out don't go unnoticed either, I can't help but be a little proud of my friend. Do not get me wrong, I have always known he was handsome, in that all-American-boy jock sort of way, but he is not for me.

"Yeah it was wicked," he replies, his cheeky grin all over his face.

"Right, that's great," I respond, knowing that he and Vicky have probably been up to something like always, but for some reason, they will not tell me. Probably because I will say it is a shit idea. *Sleeping with a friend that is.*

"You want to come out this Friday? Vicky and I are heading to The Point before hitting town.

It's day one of school and we already need alcohol. This can't be a good sign."

He laughs. "Yeah why not, I might come up and see you guys after practice."

Jesse is the captain of the basketball team and will be major famous one day for his ball skills. "Sounds good."

After saying goodbye to Jesse, I admire the tall buildings as I make my way back to the dorm.

Our college is beautiful in an old rustic way. I pull my sunglasses down over my eyes, and power walk so I can to get home and take these jeans off. I need my track pants, and I need them now.

I walk into our apartment, kick my shoes off, take off my bra, pull my hair free of its elastic and pour a glass of wine. I'm looking over my notes from the day, and must be on glass number three when Vicky walks in, looking as if she is trying to run away from someone. And when I see Jesse walking up behind her, I know why.

"Hey guys, couldn't wait for you sorry. I needed a wine."

I say, looking over to them from my cosy spot on the sofa.

Vicky drops all the grocery bags on the kitchen table.

"I'm going to need more than wine to get me through this shit," she replies. So quietly, I almost missed it. "Have a good day?" I ask with a smile, trying to cheer her up. She looks at me. "Just perfect!" she says dripping with sarcasm. I look over awkwardly at Jesse and see he looks uncomfortable. *This is exactly what I was meaning when I said don't sleep with your friends.* I think to myself, turning my attention back to my books.

It has been over an hour since Vicky and Jesse got back, and it feels as though the tension has died down a little. So we all cosy up on the couch, eating the tacos Vicky made. That girl is a mean cook; she will make someone a happy man one day.

Putting some bad chick flick on the TV, I relax into the sofa and enjoy the fatty goodness. I look over at Jesse and giggle to myself; he's always stuck with our girlie shows.

"So, I met someone during the holidays," Vicky states casually in between very big bites. I think to myself that maybe she's scoffing her face so she doesn't have to answer any more questions that she knows are coming.

"What?" I ask, taking a gulp of my wine.

Vicky does not date, ever. She does casual so I'm a little surprised.

"I don't know, I guess it's not serious, that's why I hadn't told you earlier."

She looks at me with a hint of a smile on her face, but if I look a little deeper, I see some confusion as well.

"Well spill women, I'm not going to wait forever."

I would totally wait forever, however, I'm getting impatient.

"Not much to spill really, his name's Blake. He's sexy, funny, and all things nice. But he also comes with a crazy ex-girlfriend, fucked up past, and commitment issues. He's made it clear that we can't be anything more. I'll just have to live with it."

I'm gobsmacked at this revelation. It's usually Vicky saying she doesn't want the commitment and the guys are the ones pawing at the door trying to get her to let them in. I shake my head a little before raising my wine glass to my lips.

"What the fuck?" Jesse spits, looking at her with anger etched all over his face. I take another large gulp of wine.

"Jesse, calm down. What we had wasn't serious and you knew that," Vicky responds, rolling her eyes at him.

I look between the two of them, feeling the tight tension in the air once again. *Just great.*

"Well alright, aside from this little out blast that I heard now, which by the way, I expect to hear about," I say pointing at them both before continuing. "When can I meet him?"

I can't help but return the smile as she breaks into a grin when she looks at me. "This weekend I think. He's part of Sinful Souls motorcycle club, they'll be back this weekend."

I hear Jesse scoff. "Oh, real classy, Vicky."

My thoughts drown out their bickering. I have heard about this motorcycle club, they are always suspects in missing persons all over the state, but the police never have enough evidence to pin anything on them. *Of course, she would be seeing one.*

"I can't wait to meet him," I say, squeezing her hand and I don't chance a glance at Jesse.

I see how happy she is just by the mention of his name. I make the mistake of looking to Jesse and see he's angry.

"I'm going to go, thanks for the invite, Lain." He pushes his plate further onto the table before getting up and walks towards the door.

I call after him. "Oh Jesse, don't be like that." But it's too late, he's already slammed the door. I look over at Vicky and raise my eyebrows. "You couldn't tell him before instead of spilling it all out in the open?"

She picks up her plate and takes it to the sink. "No, he needs to get it, Lain. I told him, *just casual* but like a grade A clinger, he got too attached."

I take my plate and join her in the kitchen. I have to raise my voice over the water gushing into the sink.

"In his defence though, I've heard you between these walls, and I don't blame him."

She laughs and whips me with a tea towel.

"Shut up."

After doing the dishes, we call it a night. I cannot wait to get to bed. Mondays suck, they're too far away from Fridays.

A sound wakes me from my sleep, I glance over to my alarm clock where it is reading 11:14pm. Getting up to get a glass of water, I look out the window and see a dozen or so bikes drive by. I begin making my way to the kitchen, when I see Vicky's bedroom door open with her not in her bed.

"Oh for fuck sake, this woman couldn't keep her legs closed if her life depended on it," I mumble to myself, as I put on my flip flops.

I decide to see if she is at Jesse's, hoping that maybe she decided to go and pay him a late night apology. *I sure bloody hope so.*

Opening our front door, I tiptoe out and down the corridor where I find myself stumbling over the empty beer cans. "Ugh gross, dumb college boys."

Reaching the end of the corridor, I push through the main front doors. A cool breeze prickles my skin to remind me of the lack of clothing I sleep in. Short pajama shorts and a white tank top that gives a hint of my flat tummy and hips.

My long, thick, naturally blonde, almost white hair, tied into a messy bun on the top of my head. I stop in my tracks when I see I am opposite my fellow promiscuous friend, and she is not alone. *Surprise, surprise.*

She sees me and giggles. "Lain? What are you doing?"

She has crazy eyes going on. I respond, "Me? I woke to find you not in your bed, so I went to try and find you."

She laughs before running her hand over the guy's chest. "This is Blake."

I look over to find two men standing against their black Harley's. One, I am assuming by the way his hand's clench my friend's ass, is Blake; who looks to be around six-foot, built nice, and lean. He has ash blond hair that is almost a buzz cut, but still long enough to run your hands through it; and brown, almost black eyes. I see his cheesy grin on his face. He is hot in a 'you're-cute-but-I-wouldn't-call-you-cute-to-your-face' kind of way.

"Hi, I'm Alaina," I greet, giving my best friend the 'this is not over' eyes.

"Blake," he responds with a grin before continuing. "What's that accent I can pick up there?"

If I had a dollar every time someone asked me this, I'd be a millionaire. Fifty percent of people don't know where New Zealand is, and the other fifty percent think it's a state of Australia, which is an inside joke. I think Canadians and Americans could relate.

"A Kiwi accent, I'm from New Zealand."

His eyes light up, and I know he wants to say something else, but I see Vick give him a side glare. He narrows his eyes back at Vicky before responding.

"Well okay little kiwi, this is my brother Zane," he points over to hot biker number two.

Holy sweet baby Jesus.

It feels like my world stops for a brief moment and all I can hear is my breathing, while I take him in slowly, *without trying to be too obvious.*

His whole body and energy surrounding him screams power and control, he has to be the hottest guy I've ever laid my eyes on and I feel my body respond causing me to cross my arms across my chest to stop the free display of my tank straining against my hardened nipples.

Standing a couple of inches over six-foot, roped in muscle, with dark hair that is short, but holds up nicely in natural spikes; giving him an edge. Green-hazel eyes, by the looks of it, with a square, strong jaw. He has two sleeve tattoos running up his arms, one that joins to a tattoo on his neck. Just to top all of that off? He has the longest, thick, dark, lashes you can imagine; and a damn *lip ring*. A fucking lip ring. *Holy fuck, I am in trouble.* He is the epitome of sexy alpha biker, and I find myself clenching my thighs together under his intense stare. He looks right at me, with a slow smirk creeping on to his face, revealing one perfect dimple on his left cheek. *Kill me now.* He gives me the head nod. "Zane," he says with a deep but seducing voice. *Not good, not good at all.* I better get out of here, before I say something completely inappropriate, or fall on my face.

"Alright, nice meeting you guys, Vick? I'll see you inside."

She looks between the two before saying, "They're going to come up? Is that okay? It'll just be for a little bit, I promise?"

I shoot her a quick evil glare before agreeing.

A few steps down the corridor, and a lot of trying to talk myself into this; we arrive at our apartment and I suck down the nerves as I open our front door. What was I thinking agreeing to this? We have a big two-bedroom apartment, which we are lucky to have, because there are only twelve of them on campus. You basically have to come from money to have one, and lucky for us, both Vicky and I do. But how I come from money, is a little more complicated to how Vicky does. Standing in our apartment with Zane, makes it feel tiny. Not only because of his sheer size, but because of the intimidating energy that surrounds him. Maybe it is the cut that reads Sinful Souls MC *or,* maybe it's because just below that, it reads President. A cut is the vest that you see members wear, it's the only visual identification of a member who is a part of an outlaw motorcycle club, it shows the club logo on the back as well as territorial location. I swallow hard, feeling every bit off my game.

As soon as we get in the door, Vicky leaps onto Blake like a fricking leech. They don't even stop as they both head towards her bedroom. I can't see his hands but he's doing something to have

Vick squealing like a sex-deprived rabbit. I shake my head while mumbling under my breath, "Real smooth, Vick."

I look over to sexy biker number two, who really should be number one, because he would give Blake a run for his money, any day of the week, and notice his eyes have not left me. He does a slow, but obvious sweep of my entire body as he keeps that cocky smirk on his face. His tongue slowly runs over his lower lip, nudging his lip ring. When he reaches my eyes again, he's greeted with one perfectly arched eyebrow, and a smirk to match his own. *One of these days, my fake confidence is going to get me killed.*

"Want a drink of anything?" I ask him, walking into the kitchen.

He sits down on our big L shaped lounge suite, with his legs spread out, and head cocked sideways, staring at me with that trademark smirk. *Sexy son of a bitch.* He has my pulse pumping with his eyes alone.

"Nah I'm good, babe." Babe? He just babed me. I should find that odd, but the way it rolled off his tongue laced with dark, sexy, dominance caused the vibrations to head straight to my...alright, Alaina, I'm cutting your thoughts off right now—reign it in woman.

I get a bottled water out of the fridge, and make my way back into the lounge before taking a seat to face him.

I ask him, "So, you guys ride in pairs? How cute."

Clearly it was the wrong thing to say Alaina, but my sarcasm knows no boundaries. I see his eyes narrow, he looks annoyed, but a smile plays on his lips too before he responds.

"Nope, I've just got to make sure no one dies tonight," he says with a little humour in his voice, but something tells me there is no way this man is joking.

"Sounds serious, I would hate to keep you from your duties."

He stands, and makes his way to me on the other side of the sofa. Almost like a cheetah and I'm the gazelle. He's going to eat me alive—and what's worse? I'll let him. He stops right in front of me, putting his finger under my chin to lift my head.

"I love your accent." He tilts his head, running his eyes up and down my body. "Almost as much as I love that sweet ass you carry."

It is a sweet ass, and I work hard to keep it that way. Cocking my head sideways, I look up to him.

"Well, that's lovely that you notice my 'sweet ass' and thank you by the way. But looking is as close as you'll be getting to it," I reply with a sweet smile.

"You can play hard to get all you want, babe," he says, coming closer and locking me between his arms. He leans down to my ear and whispers, "But that hot feeling you're feeling between your legs? Is for me, and me only. Your blush gives it a way, and I know you feel the same pull I feel."

He's right, my palms sweat, and my pulse picks up, just by him giving me those devilish eyes.

"Cocky are we?" I ask with a smile.

He gives me a sheepish grin before moving to sit down.

I take a sip of my water, hoping it will calm down my raging hormones. There is a big part of me that feels interested in him, not just because he is panty-dropping sexy either—well mainly that. But also because I always want to know people on a deeper level.

"I have no idea how long those two are going to be," I say, feeling awkward with our silence after that little performance.

"Why did you come outside?" he asks.

I look over to him, and see he's frowning. It looks cute on such a beast of a man.

"I was trying to find Vicky, I knew she couldn't be far at this time of night, and she sometimes goes to see our friend Jesse, who lives in the dorms across from our building," I replied. That didn't seem to settle him at all, his frown remains the same.

"You're dressed like that," he says, pointing to my pajamas; which are my favourite in this sticky California heat. He's lucky I'm wearing clothes at all. He continues. "And you're walking around late at night. You need to be more careful, it's not smart."

I take another drink and laugh. "Why would you care?"

He smiles and relaxes back to his position. "I don't, I'm just saying, from one human to another." Right, of course. Now I feel like an idiot. I stand ready to make a run for it.

"I might just go to bed, you can let yourself out."

He watches me rise from the couch before doing the same. It surprises me when he stalks over to me all while maintaining my stare. When he reaches me, he tucks a strand of hair behind my ear which causes a shudder to ripple through me, and kisses my forehead. I stand there dumbfounded as he walks out the door without a second glance. *He just, leaves.*

Aside from my complete confusion, I feel like I'm fourteen again and have never been kissed. I have never seen anyone holy shit as hot as Zane Mathews.

I crawl between the sheets and close my eyes. I take a deep shaky breath and know I'm going to have the same nightmare I've had night after night, but I drift off anyway, knowing there's no escaping it.

I'm tucked into my covers, in my bedroom when he came in.

"You will be mine, Alaina, and you will make my son happy."

I'm scared, I don't want him in my room. I can't tell anyone because he told me they won't believe me. I do not want my mom to think I was a liar. I would never lie. He brought his face down to mine, placing his hand over my mouth, squeezing tight.

"I will be back for you. You just wait. Your daddy owes me." He smiled his gold tooth grin at me. He'd made me feel dirty. Mommy always told me that if anyone touched me, I must tell her. But he'd never touched me in a perverse way, what he'd done was just as damaging. He laid claim to my soul, before it had a chance to feel what it was like to be free.

ZANE

Six Months Ago

"Prez, the lines for you."

I was sitting at the bar, trying to find a way to divorce this bitch without putting a bullet between her eyes when Ade came up to me, waving the phone.

Snatching it out of his hands, I brought it to my ear. "What?"

Today was not the day to piss me off, but I think that's pretty much every day.

"I need a favour," the voice responded.

I knew this voice, I hadn't heard it in a while though.

"What is it you need, Joseph?"

By the time our conversation was over, I was more pissed than before. If my old man and Joseph were not best friends/brothers growing up, and if Joseph wasn't the CEO of the Confederation of Assassins, I would have buried him just for asking this of me. Babysitting is in no way something I'm ever interested in, especially no hood rat with mommy and daddy issues.

I told Joseph to send me all the info he can about her, before swiping one of the sweet butts and escorting her to my bed.

After getting my dick sucked dry, I made my way to the office where the fax machine was going off. I collected all the papers that had already fallen to the ground, noticing the photos first. One of them showed her walking down the street arm in arm with a tall, leggy, brunette, laughing with her head thrown back, and big sunglasses on.

"Fuck," I muttered.

She looked so carefree and nowhere near what I'd pictured her to be. She's beautiful. Wait re-think that, I fucking never call a girl beautiful. Pulling out my seat, I sat down and continued to look through all the information, while thinking of a plan.

A couple of joints later, and after a lot of hard thinking, I stood up off my chair.

"BLAKE! In here now."

He came walking in, with a club whore on his arm.

"What can I do for you, boss?" I chuckled because he has no idea.

"Well, it's funny you ask that." Sitting forward and putting out my joint. I smirked at him, "Something just came up."

CHAPTER 2

ALAINA

Present day

I wake up in a cold sweat and glance at the alarm clock. Three a.m. Great. *I'm going to be tired tomorrow,* I tell myself as I toss and turn before drifting back to sleep.

This time, instead of waking to my alarm clock, I'm waking to the deep bass sound of Snoop Dogg's *'Wiggle.'*

I groan and put the pillow over my head. "Fuck my life." Moaning with my hair all over the place, I head out to where the nuisance is coming from. I'm greeted by my crazy best friend dancing around making pancakes with two bikers sitting on the couch. My face shows no amusement whatsoever, and I do not care how crazy I look.

"What the fuck, Vick, turn it down!" I shout to be heard.

She spins around while laughing.

"No can do, sugar. I'm on a good vibe this morning, all I want to do is dance," she replies while dropping her ass low to the floor. I narrow my eyes at her.

"You know, I love you and all that, but if you don't turn it down now, I might just cut you in your sleep." I am completely serious.

Looking over to Blake and Zane, I can see them holding in their laughs. Rolling my eyes, I go back to bed. As soon as I lay my head down, my door opens. I don't have to look to know who it is.

"You're cute when you're crazy," he says in between chuckles.

"Yeah well, I'm about to get real adorable if you don't give me my beauty sleep."

I hear him laugh before feeling the mattress dip.

"Don't you have scary biker duties to take care of?" I ask, flipping over to my back so I can face him. "Not right now, no." He leans down onto his elbows and looks into my eyes. I squirm, breaking eye contact. It's too much. He's too much.

"What are you studying?"

"You want to know what I'm studying?" I ask with an amused tone.

"Can't I be interested?" he retorts with a snark.

"You can, but it's a little shady," I reply, letting my remaining hair down out of the tight bun.

"Oh? How so?" he asks with a smirk.

"Why are you interested?"

"I don't know. The feeling is new to me. Never gave a fuck before. But you interest me."

I'm not sure if I want his attention. He's so overwhelming and I can't stop looking at his lip ring. "That's not weird at all," I mumble before continuing. "The feeling is mutual though."

"It is?" he tilts his head.

"Well, I felt that...pull you were talking about."

He picks me up as if I am as light as a feather, and places me on top, so I'm straddling him. "Tell me you want this as much as I do."

I look down on him, and there is absolutely no denying how much I want him. "I do."

Before I can blink, his mouth is connecting with mine, owning me body and soul. His kiss is fierce with lust and passion, and I think fuck it—what's *one* time.

My hands creep up, and find his hair. The large bulge pushing against my core doesn't go unnoticed either, it ignites me even more.

Before I know it, he's lifted me off the bed, wrapping my legs around his waist, as he pushes me up against the wall.

"Fuck," he moans into my mouth, pushing my top up over my head, and grazing past my perky nipple, squeezing it as he rips my tank top off. He takes a nipple in his mouth, before showing some attention to my other. *I am lost in ecstasy.* Getting back on my feet, I pull at his top, throwing it on the ground, and I can't help but stare with raw appreciation. His body is carved out of stone; with that perfect V lining right down.

I get to work on his belt buckle, and pull his pants down while getting on my knees. I fist his cock in my hand, and rub my thumb over the tip of his thick hard tip. I bring my thumb up to my mouth, and lick his pre-cum off, peering up at him from my position. I watch as his green eyes close with need. Studying his huge cock, I'm wondering how it's going to fit in my mouth, let alone in my now wet pussy.

I slide my lips over him, and take him deep in my mouth, wrapping my fingers around his length, I slowly begin to bob my head, hearing his moan slip out. I slowly lick around and down his shaft, and just as I'm getting a rhythm going, he puts his hand around my jaw, stopping me.

"The first time I come with you, will not be in your mouth."

Getting back to my feet, he pulls my pajama shorts and panties down, before sweeping his fingers in between my cleft. He looks at me with a smirk, licking me off his fingers, then rubs it around my nub, before dipping it deep into my pussy. I cry out as he curls his finger, hitting my spot. He works me up until I'm just about to give way to an orgasm, he pulls his fingers out, grabs a condom wrapper out of his pocket, biting it open with his teeth and sliding it down his long, thick, dick.

He grips my hips and picks me up again to slam into me in one hard thrust. He starts slowly, but forcefully, pounding me against the wall. *I'm seeing stars.* I have never been fucked like this before, it's pure, deep, hard fucking. I can feel myself building higher and higher, until I am right at my peak. "Come, baby," he says, bringing his hand between us, rubbing my throbbing clit, pushing him and me over. My body jerks as the aftershocks surge through my body, *holy fuck.*

He pulls out of me, putting me back on my feet and tying up the condom, before throwing it in the bin. "Well, that's one unexpected way to wake up," I say as I wrap the sheet around me, feeling a little naked.

I know Vick would have heard all that too, I will no doubt get the inquisition from her later.

"Unexpected for you maybe." He winks at me.

It's then that I realise what I have done, and I blush with embarrassment. I cannot trust myself around Zane; he ignites a flame in me that just wants to burn forever.

He must see the confliction on my face. I have been told that I am very transparent, but I keep a lot locked inside of me as well, only Vicky knows my darkest of secrets.

Sensing what I am about to say, he interrupts my thoughts.

"I'm not leaving, get in the bathroom and I'll clean you up."

For some stupid reason, I start following him to the bathroom. *What the fuck is wrong with my body; it has a mind of its own where Zane is concerned.*

He pulls out a towel, and runs it under the water. "Sit." I pull down the toilet lid, and do as I am told. He begins to clean around my thighs, he looks up at me under those lashes. It is then when something clicks.

"What the hell?" I yell, shooting up mortified. "You wore a condom! I saw you put one on."

Looking at me, he smirks. "This isn't me babe, this is all you, and it's all *mine.*"

Apparently I make a mess when I have a Zane Mathews induced orgasm. Sitting back down, all I want to do it is cry. I feel like I have disappointed myself, but being around Zane feels right. Which makes no sense, because I barely know him.

"I'm tired Zane, I didn't get much sleep last night."

He drops the towel in the basket, picks me up, and cradles me against his chest, while walking back into my room, and kicking the door shut behind him.

He places me in my bed, jumps in behind me, and pulls me in close, so I'm spooning him. "Um, Zane?" I ask, feeling like I have no idea what the hell just happened.

"Shh, Alaina, don't think too much into it, just sleep," he replies, deep into my ear.

And I do, I drift off not worrying about the nightmares to come.

ZANE

This girl has me all kinds of fucked up. I've known her personally for less than twenty-four hours, and she has already managed to ease her way under my skin. There's just something about her, I knew that when I saw her photos for the first time that I wanted her. Jesus, even her photos alone had my dick standing to attention. Those photos, they don't do her justice. It's probably because she's so fucking beautiful, but yet still so innocent looking. On the other hand, maybe it's her smart mouth that has me on edge. Whatever it is, I need to cut the shit. I need to keep her at a distance, what just went down twenty minutes ago, can never happen again. I'm sure pounding her pussy up against her bedroom wall, was not part of the job description.

I look down to her sleeping form, not wanting to leave her. She looks so innocent, and vulnerable, an intense need to protect her from anything and anyone takes over my body.

"Fuck," I mumble, realising I may just be in this too deep. Brushing her hair out of her face, I kiss her head, and then slowly make my way off the bed, throwing my clothes back on. When I walk out of her room, her best friend Vicky is leaning against the wall with her arms crossed in front of her.

"If you hurt her—" I cut her off by raising my hand, because quite frankly, I don't give a fuck what she has to say. "You will do nothing, because you can't. And what I do with her, is none of your business." I walk past her.

"Like fuck I'll be settling for that as an answer!"

Her words don't stop me as I carry on walking, *fucking bitches.*

"Just remember one thing, Zane," she yells from her door as I continue on down the hallway. "You're not the only one who sleeps with a nine under their pillow." I stop and glance over my shoulder, throwing her a smirk before walking out the door.

To be honest, I'm impressed. Not only is the girl hot, but she holds her own. She's lucky Blake has created little fluffy feelings for her, or I would have taken that last little comment as a threat.

Jumping on my bike, I head back to the clubhouse with one girl on my mind.

ALAINA

I wake up a couple of hours later, feeling very much content with myself, wondering why I feel so sedated, until the memories come splashing back to me.

"Oh my god," I cringe to myself, putting my hand over my mouth with embarrassment while I rub my thighs together, savoring the delicious sting.

My door flies open, and I'm expecting to see my current mistake walk through, but it's not, it's a certain fiery brunette.

"Speak. Now," she says, pointing to the floor.

"I'm pretty sure I don't need to tell you anything. I think you heard it all this morning," I say getting up and making my way to the bathroom.

"Yes, I did. I don't know, Lain. I don't know if this is a good idea. Blake says he's the tap and gap kind of person. Not the clean you up and lay your head down type."

I think she is being a little dramatic because he did just that. He did clean me up and lay my head down this morning, but I won't tell her that.

"Vicky, calm down, we were both tired is all." I'm not about to tell her that it's because we fucked each other senseless.

"It won't happen again, I've got to keep my head in my studies."

She laughs while walking out my door. "Lain, you can study and still get fucked at the same time. By the way, this was here for you." She hands me a small box with a ribbon and waits for me to open it. Surely this isn't a gift for sex. I open it to find a necklace with a green stone known as Kawakawa pounamu. It's a small pendant piece of the stone on a gold chain. The dark flecks throughout make it look stormy.

"Was there a note?" I ask.

"Only the one with your name on it. Found it on the coffee table. It's gorgeous." She takes it from my hands and fastens the clasp. My fingers touch the cool stone and I can't help but think of home.

I turn the shower on, still shaking my head thinking of Vicky's final comment. Scrubbing up quickly, I throw on some cut-offs and a shirt before gathering my books. The hot California sun warms me instantly when I step outside as I make my way to my first class.

I'm rounding the car park, thinking about a certain man in leather, when I see a black Mercedes car parked under a tree. It has black mag wheels and blacked out lights. My first thought was that's a little flashy to be here, but then I think nothing of it as there are hundreds of cars parked here every day. Realising I have been staring a little too long, I look away, and then they suddenly pull out and take off fast.

"Weird," I mutter to myself.

"What's weird?" Jesse asks, coming up behind me.

"Oh no, it's nothing, how are you feeling? I'm sorry about Vick."

He laughs my comment off. "Don't apologise for her, Lain, I guess she's right, I did fall a little deep for her."

I snatch his basketball out of his hands and start bouncing it while we walk.

"I love her more than anything, but I still think she should've let you know on your own."

He shrugs his shoulders, swiftly taking the ball back, and I stop in surprise. "Oh don't sulk, Lain, we'll start our training again if you want."

While he's distracted with his talk of training me to play ball, I snatch it out of his grasp and run. I hear him laughing before yelling at me.

"Cheat move, Lainy,"

So I flip him the bird in response, because I'm mature like that.

By the end of the day, I am beat. All I want to do is sleep, but I know I need to burn some calories off; thanks to that donut my inner fat bitch decided she wanted for lunch.

I put on my running shoes, plug in my beats, and head out my jog.

Saving Abel's *'Addicted'* comes blasting through my ears, reminding me of my events last night. *Nope, not going there.* Therefore, I quickly change the song to something more upbeat.

I have just found my running pace, and I round the corner just before the footpath along the beach, when I notice the same car following slowly behind me. I don't look straight away, because I don't want them to think I've noticed them. Instead, I decide to run to where I know Vicky is with Blake, at a bar down the street.

I keep up my pace, while trying not to go into a full blast run. Checking out my surroundings, I see there are a few people out and about for a Thursday afternoon. *Alaina - 1, scary car people - 0.*

I see Billy Joe's lights flashing ahead, so I run directly to it until I crash open the doors. I notice it is empty, aside from Vicky and Blake sitting in front of the bar. No one knows about my past except Vicky, not even Jesse.

"Lain, babe what's wrong?" Vicky asks, walking right up to me.

I flick my eyes at Blake, who looks a bit off guard. A crazy girl runs through a bar with him being here on his own with no back up, I see it has him on edge as he tries to look over my shoulder to the door.

"Vick, a car has been following me, I saw it today on campus, then just now while I was out on my run. It was following behind me, so I kept my pace normal, hoping they didn't know I noticed them," I burst out.

She pales and her eyes go wide.

"Do you think? Do you think this has to do with your parents?"

CHAPTER 3

I'm pacing up and down the bar thinking about her question. I always knew it was a possibility that I would be found, but now that it's real, I can feel myself slowly start to panic.

"I don't know. I don't see why else I would be getting followed."

Blake stands up, and starts to walk outside, then comes back in.

"Black Mercedes? Still here across the street. I'm going to call Zane."

Oh no, I start to shake my head. "No please don't, I don't want to be that annoying girl after a one night stand." I almost beg him.

"Babe, you will never be that annoying girl after a one night stand. Besides, you need hooker heels for that," he replies with a grin before continuing. "I have to call this in." He walks off, mumbling with hushed tones into his phone.

I turn to Vicky. "Vick, people are going to begin to find out about my past."

She takes hold of my hand. "I know. It's going to be okay though. You are not going anywhere." If only that were true.

Fifteen minutes later, I hear a swarm of bikes pull up outside, and my butterflies start acting up again. I can't believe I'm going to see him again, under the worst circumstances. Lucky I'm in my best yoga pants and sports bra, but nothing is going to cover the beads of sweat dripping all over my face and body. *Charming, Alaina.*

The doors swing open, and a very angry Zane strolls in, with me in his direct line of fire and I can't help but recoil from him. I see him do a full sweep of my body as he comes strolling over to me with his jaw clenching. I almost think that I'm in trouble, then he picks me up like I weigh nothing, and kisses me so passionately, I turn to instant mush in his arms.

When he has put me down, I notice all eyes on us. I count seven big, burly, bikers who are watching us; they are not scary in a creepy, pervy, way because they were all really good looking. Which is surprising for a MC, or maybe I just watch too many movies where they stereotype all bikers to come complete with a beer belly, long unkempt hair, and beards with last night's meal still on them. *And by meal, I mean all things you can eat.*

"I hope the staring is because of that kiss I just laid down, and not my girl in her non-existent gym clothes," he calls over his shoulder and they all look away with a few laughs.

"Baby, what's happening?" he asks, and I tell him about the car following me. "Any reason why?" looking deep into my eyes, but throwing sideway glances at the boys as well.

"There maybe one or two reasons, yes," I respond nervously.

I've never spoken to anyone apart from Vicky about my past before.

"I haven't had the smoothest childhood." And I tell him everything, from the beginning about how the last memory I have of my mother is her hurrying me out my window.

He looks at me with a hint of sadness in his eyes.

"I'm sorry, babe, do you know who this man is that your father owed?"

I know who's behind it, but I don't want to involve Zane into my drama. I have always known that this day would come, that I would need to pack up and relocate. I was just hoping it would wait until after I finished school.

"No, look it's fine. I know what I have to do, and I've prepared myself for this moment since I was eight." He looks at the rest of the men, and for a second, I forgot I had an audience.

He looks back at me before he says, "You're coming back to the clubhouse, until we sort this out."

The men all look at him and nod, but the older one of the group says, "Are you sure this is a good idea Z, bringing on shit that has nothing to do with us, it doesn't sound smart."

I rest my hand over his, he has a point. It's not their war. "He's right," I say to Zane as he scowls at the man while I nod at him in understanding.

"I wasn't asking for permission, brother, her war became mine the moment I stuck my dick in her." My hand stills on his. *Well, as far as bluntness goes, I would say that takes the cake.*

One of the other men, who appears to be around the same age as Zane, smiles at me.

"It's nice to meet you, sweetheart, I'm Ade. Any enemy of Bianca, is a friend of mine."

I look at him a little confused, then look to Zane who is shooting daggers at him. Ade's sexy in a pretty boy with piercings and tattoos kind of way. He has a warmness about him, even though he is built like Hulk. And I feel an instant bond with him.

"Nice to meet you Ade, but who is Bianca?" he laughs, and is just about to open his mouth when Zane steps in.

"Drop it, Ade," he growls.

Ade throws me a wink before getting a drink from the bar. Yep, we are going to get on really well.

I'm still smiling at him, when I notice Zane looking between Ade and me with an icy stare. "Pack your shit, Alaina, you have two hours."

I raise my eyebrow at him, "Snappy much?" His jaw ticks, so I decide now is probably a good time to leave.

"I'll meet you back at mine," I respond, as I head out of the bar.

I know I should be grateful because this isn't his burden, but the man is demanding and controlling. I've already told him that he didn't need to do this, and I can't see why he would do it either; something doesn't add up.

A noise behind me gets my attention and I turn to see Zane walking up to me.

"Stop, Alaina, stop trying to run."

"I'm not trying to run, Zane, I'm just trying to understand why you're willing to put your life, and your brothers lives, on the line for little old me, who you've only known for one night!"

"I can't explain it to you right now, even though I want to, but you're just going to have to trust me. And you're right, I wouldn't throw the lives of my brothers down for you, no matter how different you may seem to me. But just know that I can't talk about this right now, so just trust me."

"The crazy thing is, I do feel like I can trust you. Which makes no fucking sense because I barely know you," I reply, throwing my hands up. "I mean, you give me this necklace. Don't you think it's a bit full on?"

"Necklace?" His eyes drop to the stone hanging from my neck.

It's not from him. I shake my head and tell him not to worry about it. I knew it was too good to be true. I want to fight it, but I listen, because at the end of the day, he hasn't given me a reason not to trust him.

I squash down my thoughts and disappointment, and take the helmet out of his hands. After putting it on, I throw my leg over behind him, trying not to be too obvious about the effect being this close to him has on me, it stirs me instantly; like he has a direct hotline to my G-spot that he can dial with one sexy stare.

I try to hold on to his hips, but he pulls me by my legs so I'm right up against his back. All I can feel are his tight abs, and ripped back beneath his cut. He is wearing his usual, white T-shirt, jeans that hang nice and loose, his cut, and black combat boots.

He has too much sexy for one woman to handle, but then thinking about Ade's comment, it sounds like I'm not the only women. I actually know nothing about this man. All I know is we have immense chemistry, and he makes me horny without so much as laying a finger on me. I want to change that as soon as possible. The rumble of the bike doesn't help my dirty thoughts either, and feeling the wind whip on my face through the loud roar of his Harley, it makes me feel free, *I think I want one.* Then I'm reminded of my co-ordination skills and think, hmm...maybe not.

Once we finally reach my dorm, I try to casually get off the bike, but fail miserably when I trip over my two left feet. *I was waiting for them to make an appearance.* He rushes off to pick me up and when he does, I see the annoyance in his eyes at my clumsiness.

"Can you watch what you're doing for two seconds without almost hurting yourself?" he snaps, looking deep into my eyes.

Our faces are so close that I can feel his breath on my lips, so I look up at them practically begging him to kiss me, and just as I close my eyes, I feel him pull back.

"I shouldn't have let us get this deep, we need to keep this clean and not do that again," he says, making me confused—*again.*

I thought we had a thing, I'm not naïve, I know that he isn't the relationship type.

"I don't get it, why are you helping me then if you're in no way interested in me on any level?" I don't try to hide the look of rejection on my face.

Deciding I want answers, and I want them now, I continue. "I want answers Zane, and you're going to give me them now, or I'm not coming." My response is childish, I know, but nothing at all makes sense to me. He looks at me clearly annoyed by my words.

"Listen, Alaina, first of all, you will be coming with me, whether you want to or not. Secondly, I don't have to tell you shit." I flinch at the harshness of his words. His hand lifts to gently brush my unruly hair out of my face. "But I want to tell you. I want you to know but I know you're going to have questions that I can't answer." He closes his eyes for a second before returning his gaze back to me. "Your father sent us to protect you. Your father is alive, Alaina.

He drops his bombshell and walks away from me. He heads towards my dorm entrance while I'm lost for words. I'm completely lost for words, then a ton of emotions come crashing down on me. His answer didn't give me any satisfaction at all. In fact, it's left me with more questions than I had before.

I can't believe my dad is alive. Where is he now? Why hasn't he come to see me? Where has he been all these years? Is mom alive too? I have more questions, but I know he's not going to answer them, at least not right now. Therefore, I follow him up to my apartment and shutting the door behind me.

"How? How did this all happen?" My hand wraps around his bicep and slow his steps. "I thought I met you by chance. I thought I meet you because Vick was sleeping with Blake?" My brain feels like it's going to seize with information. He takes my keys from my hand and opens the door.

He starts to walk to my bedroom. "Blake had a job to do, get with Vicky, to get us to you." Now I'm pissed off, they used my best friend's feelings as a gateway to get to me.

"You're telling me, Blake doesn't *actually* like Vicky? That it was all set up, and she doesn't know!" My voice rises because I'm fuming.

He steps up to me with an annoyed look on his face. "Oh I can assure you, we've done much, *much* worse than your little college drama. And yes, that's exactly what I'm saying. Now pack your shit. We are leaving in twenty."

I can't believe it. I can't wait to have words with Blake, that sneaky shit.

"I thought you said I had two hours?" Ignoring me, he carries on with pulling my clothes out of my drawers.

"You did, but then you pissed me off, so I changed my mind. Don't push me, Alaina, I don't have time for it." This Zane is so cold and distant and the playful man I met a few days ago, is gone, now it's all business.

"Fine," I say quietly, and a little hurt. *Of course he wouldn't be interested in me by choice.*

I had one more question to ask him, then I would leave it alone *for now.* "Did you want to fuck me that night or was that all just part of the plan?"

His hands still mid-air wrapped around my T-shirts. He looks at me, and I wonder whether he sees the tiny bit of emotion on my face. After his brief pause, he goes back to what he was doing, "Part of the plan." His words feel like a punch to the stomach. I've never felt so used before.

I walk into my wardrobe, grab my gym bag and fill it up with clothes. I go a little heavy on the underwear, because next to my gym clothes addiction, is my Victoria Secret shopping addiction. Sexy underwear always makes me happy, and the way I'm feeling right now, I need me some happy.

I can see him in the corner of my eye, watching me carefully. He opens his mouth,

Amo Jones

about to say something, but then closes it while I'm zipping up my bag.

I calm my crazy enough to say, "You don't have to explain yourself to me Zane, you don't owe me anything. I get it."

I don't. I definitely do not think sleeping with me was necessary, but I don't want to sound like a crazy, demanding, psycho, bitch either. I'm a 'suffer in silence' type, showing emotion means showing him I care, and he doesn't deserve that.

He looks at me in shock, as if he was expecting me to flip out. *Yeah right buddy, not going to happen.* Now I just want a beer and answers.

CHAPTER 4

ZANE

Yeah, I'm a fucking liar, so what. I have done worse things in this world. Slipping my cock into the daughter of the most notorious assassin known to mankind—not smart, but I'm not going to pretend that I haven't been pining after her since the first day I saw her pictures six months ago. That's six months she has basically had my balls on a leash without any knowledge. I don't bow down to anyone—ever, but I'd wipe my ass across the concrete just to see her come undone at the hands of me. The fucking girl is out of this world. She's innocent without being naive and bad enough to hold her own. She may not know it yet, but there is fire under that silky skin. She's cool, calm and collected, but I see it, I see that I have pissed her right off with my comment.

"Alaina, I need you to trust me, do you trust me?" I ask, handing her clothes.

"What am I meant to say, Zane? Yes? Yes I trust you yet you're mood swings are like riding a fucking rollercoaster!" she replies, shoving more shit in her bag before zipping it up. Yeah, I can't do this with her, not yet. So I shut my mouth, pick up her now packed bag and head straight for the door.

"Come on, we need to go," I demand, gripping onto the door knob.

"Zane?" her sweet voice asks from behind me. "Will you keep me safe?"

My eyes close and my fist clench in frustration. Frustration that she even has to ask me that, frustration that she doesn't know just how much I fucking like her. I open my eyes, keeping them fixed on the maroon wall in front of me.

"Yes, Alaina. Yes I will look after you," I answer as I carry on out the door with her following close behind me. *And I will destroy anyone who comes near you.*

CHAPTER 5

ALAINA

Pulling up to the clubhouse, I take in my surroundings. It is exactly how you would picture a clubhouse to look, only nicer. The whole place is fenced in with a high gate, and a string of barbwire running along the top. To the left, is a giant building with a large deck, which leads into what looks like a bar. To the right, there's a large ten door garage, with a line of motorbikes parked in front. *Oh I feel very safe, thanks a lot dad.*

I jump off the bike much more deftly than the first time, handing my helmet to Zane. "Ready to meet everyone?" he asks, while putting my helmet back on the bike. "I want you to remember one thing though," he says, walking toward me with complete seriousness in his expression. "These people are not your friends, Alaina, they are bikers. They are raw and some of them are killers."

I try not to look shocked by his explaining of the men I'm about to be basically living with until this all blows over. My poker face is strong.

"None of them will touch you, because they take orders from me. But know this, I don't want you doing anything with any of them. This is business only, there will be no fucking going on, do you understand me?" he proceeds to walk up to me until I feel his lips touch my ear. "If you feel the need to be fucked, you come to my door and my door only. Are we understood?"

Knowing my father is the reason I'm here and not for any other reason, I can't help but snicker at his demands. Feeling rebellious, I push the boundary further.

"That's some big speech, *Prez,* but I can assure you, there will be no knocking on your door, horny or not."

He smirks but the glare is not lost on me. "We'll see."

I start to follow him as we make our way onto the porch, I can hear a lot of yelling and music. I suddenly feel nervous.

Pulling open the door, I decide to have a quick look around before people notice we're here. To the right, there is a long bar that probably seats the whole club. On the far left side, there are two pool tables with two sofas around them. But the part that attracts me the most about this impressive layout, is that in between the pool tables and the bar, there is a mini catwalk lined with little light bulbs and a stripper pole at the end. *Shit,"* I mumble to myself under my breath. It's much, *much,* more luxurious than what I pictured it to be.

I follow Zane to the bar, where most of the men are sitting, with a few barely clothed whores on their lap. *Gross, I'll need an STI check, just for breathing the same air as these 'girls'.*

Once I finish my evaluation, I notice everyone looking towards us.

I see Ade, and give him a polite smile. His face lights up with a smile creeping across it; giving me a wink. Our little greeting is interrupted, when I feel the tight squeeze on my arm, looking up to find Zane glaring at me *again.* With his jaw ticking. I widen my eyes in a silent protest before turning back to continue what I was doing, *perving at Ade.*

"This is Alaina, she'll be staying with us until some shit blows over, you all know the deal with her old man, so I don't need to repeat myself. She'll be staying in the spare room upstairs." He looks at all the men, before adding. "And she's off limits."

I hear a lot of moaning and groaning, which sees my self-esteem jump a bit. After getting battered down by Zane earlier, it needed the boost. *Jeez Alaina, that's an all-time low, bikers will fuck anything,* I briefly think to myself.

Looking around the bar, I notice that this isn't your average looking motorcycle club. I mean, when one thinks of a motorcycle club, one tends to think of, stinky, old men, with beer guts and missing teeth. But not this group of men. *Holy fuck.* My inner self is suddenly excited. *The perverted bitch.* Even in age, the oldest man here would have to be around forty-five, and he is a good looking forty-five-year-old. He looks shockingly similar to Daniel Craig.

The rest of them aren't anywhere near their forties, and they are all different kinds of sexy, in their rough, raw, fucked up, bad boy, sort of ways.

Zane looks at me, then points down the line starting with Daniel Craig. He begins the introductions. "Felix." Felix gives me, what looks like a small smile. *Mr Serious.*

He carries on. "Harvey." I would say early thirties, with longish, dark, hair, that hangs naturally around his collar, and bright blue eyes. He has a natural sex appeal about him, while noting he's a rough looking Jared Leto; my inner fourteen year old self jumps in glee, not because I want to jump his bones, but because I was a huge 30 Seconds to Mars fan as a teen.

He grabs a beer off the bench before continuing, "Ollie," he says after taking a swig of beer. I pull my hungry eyes off Zane to get back to introductions. Ollie looks to be around Zane's age, in his late twenties maybe early thirties. Very sharp features with a strong jaw. I was about to say he's handsome, until I notice the scar that goes across his left eye. He's still handsome, but in a very rough, masculine, way.

Zane spits, "You know Ade." I look to see Ade looking at me with a mischief smirk that would have any girl's blood pumping. He's packing some serious charm. I'm talking, a sexy face, placed on a six foot three-inch body, that is covered in tattoos and a few piercings here and there.

I look at the next person in line, while Zane points his bottle in his direction. "Chad." I'm thinking he's in his mid-thirties, and I'd put money down that he's ex-military. He smiles at me, and tilts his drink up with a nod. *He seems friendly enough.*

"Those four are prospects," he says, pointing to the sofas by the pool tables. "And they're not important right now, all you have to know, is that they're there if you need anything." He looks back at me before continuing, "And if you need to

go anywhere, one of them will be going with
you."

He places his empty bottle down, before
picking up a new one. "Come, I'll take you to your
room, got some shit to sort tonight." Fine by me,
having him around me makes me nervous. It will
be nice to just be in my own space.

I follow him around the back of the bar, where
there is a flight of stairs. Once we reach the top,
we take a right turn, leading us to the very end.
"That's where I'll be sleeping," he says pointing
to a door before pointing to a second. "And this is
where you will be sleeping."

Walking into the room, there is not much to it,
but it's not run down either. A double bed sits in
the middle of the room facing the door, with two
bedside drawers on either side. "Bathroom is
third door down to your left," he says looking
slightly agitated.

I start to fidget as I feel the hostility. "Did I do
something wrong?"

He looks down at me, catching my wondering
eyes while I'm admiring him. He really is a giant
of a man, looking into his hazel, green eyes in
awe. And while I'm drooling, he's scowling.
"Don't look at me like that Alaina, unless you
want to get fucked," snapping me out of my pervy
state. I wonder to myself, how many times a girl
needs to be turned down, before she loses all

faith in men. With her self-esteem in shambles, resorts to owning one hundred cats while having date nights in with Vibrator Bob and getting off to cheap porn currently airing on cable.

Realising I need to get my head in the game, because I'm sick of his mood swings. I open my mouth to respond, but he hooks his finger under my chin, tilting my head up to face him. "I won't be long," and by surprise, he kisses me softly on the lips.

"What?" I ask, turning to him as he's walking out. "What was that?"

He turns to me, giving me a full blown, showing lots of straight teeth smile, and flashing not one, but two perfect dimples that lay on his gorgeous face. It really is not fair how beautiful this man is, he needs to be on the cover of a magazine, possibly one about controlling, dominant, alpha males. "*That* was me saying to behave yourself," he says before walking out the door. When did my life become so damn complicated?

Looking at my phone, I notice how late it is. I gather up my pajamas and make my way to the bathroom, after realizing I need a shower. After getting there in one piece, I quickly lock it before stripping off and hopping into the bath. I turn the shower on to scorching hot, hoping that will clear my head, but it doesn't, it just gives me more time to think and create more questions.

I get out of the shower, dry off, and put on my pajamas which consist of little white silk shorts and a yellow singlet, before making my way back to my room. I decide I need to text Jesse knowing he'll be worried. Knowing him and Vicky, they wouldn't have spoken since their little bust up.

> Me: *Hey J, just checking in with you. I'm staying with a friend for a bit, so I'll see you when I get back.*

I put my phone on the side table so I can make a start on hanging my clothes. Before I get halfway to the wardrobe, my phone pings. I slide it open to see a reply from Jesse.

> Jesse: *Hey Lain, are you okay? What's going on? I saw Vicky earlier, we didn't make eye contact but I could see she was upset about something. She was a mess, don't know what's going on with her and the biker.*
> Me: *What? This MC is going to be a man down if he keeps up this shit, and yes I'm fine, just some family issues.*

Coming to think of it, I didn't see Blake downstairs earlier. He's probably at home. Do they even have homes? Or do they just all live here.

> Jesse: *I do not doubt your level of craziness, try and stay safe and text me if you need anything.*
> Me: *Will do xo.*

Dropping my phone onto the bed, I begin to tie my hair in a high messy bun and make my way to the kitchen, because being hungry sucks. I walk in and see an older woman there, she must be in her mid-fifties. She's beautiful, and has a gentleness in her features that greets me straight away.

"You must be Alaina, I'm Annabel, Zane's mother," she says with a warm smile on her face. She has shoulder length blonde hair and a tiny petite figure.

"Oh," I say surprised and a little uncomfortable. "Hello, nice to meet you." I smile back at her. She looks and seems normal. I wonder why Zane is obviously so emotionally shut down.

"Are you hungry? There's some leftover chicken in the fridge from last night, I could make you a sandwich?" she asks, looking to me while making her way to the fridge.

"Thank you, but you don't need to do that. You sit down," I answer, getting up to begin on my sandwich.

"I know you're father, quite well actually."

I stop in the middle of putting a heavy amount of mayonnaise on my bread. *High cholesterol save.* "Can I ask how?" she smiles at me while touching her chest.

"You can, he was my late husband's best friend." I gasp at the realization that Zane's dad and her husband is dead. All these years, I've held onto the hope that my parents were alive but I think somewhere along the way, I had to consider that they weren't.

She continues, "I'm really sorry for what happened all those years ago Alaina, if David was still alive, he would have made sure you were well taken care of," she adds, taking a sip of her coffee. Before I can tell her that it's fine, the rest of my childhood wasn't that bad, she continues. "This Club is a family business, we take care of family. You have nothing to be afraid of."

I take a seat opposite her on the table, taking a bite out of my sandwich. "I think your son may think otherwise."

She continues to look at me, a little longer than what is necessary before replying, "Yes, I do believe he may. I see the way he stiffens at the mention of your name."

I stop chewing and shake my head, "Only because he's annoyed by my presence, *and* his current babysitting duties." I get up to rinse my plate, putting it in the dishwasher. "Thank you for the sandwich, now I'm going to find something with vodka in it. It's been one of those days."

Squeezing her hand in appreciation, she smiles genuinely back at me. "I'll leave you to it," she replies, before adding, "Just watch those club whores, they have claws the size of a tiger."

Did she just say whores?

I laugh. "So do I." I wink at her, while she quietly laughs to herself.

I start to make my way towards the bar, hoping I don't get lost. Once I find it, I see Ade sitting on one of the stools, drinking on his own. So I make my way towards him, with vodka on my mind.

He turns to see me. "How you going, little kiwi?" I think that name has stuck with most people.

I sink down onto the seat next to him. "Not good, I need vodka to make me better."

He nods his head in understanding, then he walks behind the bar, pulling a top shelf bottle down and pouring me a glass.

"Perfect," I smile, as he sits back down next to me.

"Feel like telling me a bit about you? Only seems fair considering, I'm supposed to dive in front of a bullet for you; should the problem arise." I look over to him in surprise, when I see he's smiling at me. *Prick*. But aside from that, he looks interested. Therefore, I tell him my story, the parts I remember and understand that is. Being hurried out of my home by my mother to my waiting aunt. I added a few bits, here and there, because I feel like sharing.

"And you haven't heard from your parents since?" he asks me under confused eyes.

"Nope, I haven't. I've just always assumed the worst you know, that they were both dead." I look closely at him, he really is beautiful. He could be a model. Everything is perfect, and his nose ring and two lip rings sitting next to each other are the cherry on the top.

"Well, your father is not, and I'm not sure about your mother," he replies, taking a sip of his drink. I nod, not wanting to push any more questions onto him.

I know how these men are, their loyalty runs thick, and besides, I want to lighten the mood, so I change the subject. "Any of these fine young whore's yours?" I ask, smiling innocently at him.

"Ha. Ha. No, not any here anyway. I prefer to get my own the old fashioned way," I raise my eyebrows in surprise. I would think any man with these girls walking around, would take advantage of the situation. They are in no way cheap looking, if anything, they are very stunning; it is a damn shame about their morals.

"Hmm, and what way would that be?" I ask, taking a drink of my vodka, but maintaining eye contact.

"The way that has them drinking vodka at the bar, while pouring out their life story," he says with a perfect dimpled smirk.

I can't help but laugh. I'm one of those awkward girls where whenever a guy hits on me, I always think they're not being serious. Ade is funny and adorable, and on any other day, *probably the day before I met Zane;* I would be purring at his offer. But I can't, realistically, I only want Zane. My desire is a complete waste of time, considering he doesn't want me.

I am on my fifth glass of vodka and feeling a little more than tipsy. I feel broken, reckless, and used. "Care to dance?" I ask, wiggling my eyebrows and putting my hand out to him.

He laughs while grabbing my hand. "Let's see what you've got, little K," pulling me to the dance floor. I may have problems walking with my two left feet sometimes, but I can definitely dance.

A lot of drinking and dancing later, I find myself on the catwalk stage, dancing and grinding on the pole, with Disturbed's *'Stricken'* booming through the speakers. I look to see Ade sitting back in front of me, taking sips out of his bottle, smirking, with his legs spread out in front of him, enjoying the show.

I'm laughing down at him, until I see movement by the porch door. Ade's head snaps up to see who it is probably thinking it's Zane. The sad thing is it's everybody, *but* Zane enjoying the show. "Come on my little go-go dancer, we gotta bounce, before you get me killed." The last thing I remember is him picking me up and carrying me to bed.

CHAPTER 6

ZANE

Leaving her in that room after seeing her eye fuck the shit out of me, has to be one of the hardest things I have done. It instantly puts me in a bad mood. I hate that I feel something for this girl, but I have to go and pay someone a little visit.

After chasing the details of the Mercedes, it came up with stolen plates. So I got my hands on the CCTV footage from outside the bar, and managed to send the photos to Joseph, who had one of his minions get the name and address of the driver.

This brings me to now, walking towards the front door of a single story average house, with Blake and Ollie following close behind me.

Amo Jones

I pull my gun out, and kick the door in. Ollie and Blake go in first with their shotguns aimed. Someone fires from my left side, just missing my shoulder, so I fire back while running for cover. After we fire a few rounds each, we wait for them to retaliate. Once we know we are in the clear, we run up to the man who is in his early fifties with a greying beard, and I clock him once with my gun, knocking him out cold.

"Z, maybe you hit him too hard," Blake laughs.

"He's still alive." I kick his chair that we have tied him to. "Wake the fuck up."

He begins to moan, and slowly open his eyes. Once they've focused on us, he flips out, pulling at the ties I put on around his wrists and legs. *Why the fuck they keep doing that, I don't know; those knots are not coming out.*

"Where is he?" I demand from him.

He starts moaning under the duct tape again, so I rip it off his mouth. "Scream and I'll shoot you without thinking twice." I bend down to meet his level, "Now, where is Shane Amaro?"

He spits to the floor and chuckles. "I'm not telling you shit, pretty boy."

I join his laugh as I begin to stand. I then pull my knife out, and stab his hand down to the chair. "Now, I can torture you all night, and trust me, it would give me tremendous pleasure. But I don't have time. I would rather just cut my losses and kill you, I'll find another source."

I start lifting my gun up to his forehead, and he must see the look of pure evil in my eyes. "I DON'T KNOW! I WAS JUST THE DRIVER!" he screams in a panic while sweat drips down his forehead.

I bend down and smile but keep my gun trained on him. "You've got to give me something better than that?"

"Uh uh," he stutters, trying to think of any information he can give me. "The warehouse on the port. It's where we always met his men to relay information."

I cock my head to the side before asking, "And with this, Information? Were you planning on using it to hurt Alaina Vance?"

He looks at me, dropping his eyes in defeat. "Yes." That's all I needed to hear, before I pull the trigger on my gun, shooting him right between the eyes, spraying the walls with his blood.

I stand there motionless for a couple of seconds. "Like fuck you are."

I put my gun and knife safely away before looking over to Ollie and Blake. Blake being the first to say something; this doesn't surprise me, he's always had more mouth than sense. "A bit extreme don't you think, Prez?" laughing at the now dead body.

"I did what I had to do," I reply simply, with not a single regret in my decision.

We're walking back out to our bikes when I start dialling Abby's number, just to give her a heads up. Abby's the chief of police. She wasn't an officer long before she got the position, which works in our favour, because she's in our pocket; and has been since she was in diapers. It is off the record, so anyone outside of our world doesn't know this; but she was raised in the arms of the motorcycle club as a kid. She's like a kid sister to all of us, or big sister to some. One of the founding brothers raised her, along with my Dad, Blake's Dad, and Ade's Dad, who are also founding brothers, after she had a rough round in the system.

"Zane, seriously?" is the first thing she says when she picks up.

"I'm sorry, baby girl," I reply, and I hear her sigh over the line.

"Okay, I'll handle it."

Lucky she has a lot of reach, this girl knows people in all aspects of life. She is not to be messed with. "Come by the clubhouse this weekend, we're having a cookout."

The line goes quiet for a while. "Yep will do, I miss you all." I smile, because there is not a thing I wouldn't do for this girl. "We miss you too."

After hanging up the call, I look over to Ollie; he is a man of hardly any words, it has a lot to do with a deadly night a few years ago. "Abby?" he asks sadly.

"The one and only, brother. You need to talk to her again, one way or another." He nods his head and grunts, typical Ollie behaviour.

We were on our way back, when I realised I needed to gas up, so we pull over at the nearest station. I am halfway through filling up, when my phone rings.

"Zane?" I would call her my wife, but she doesn't deserve that title. Bianca purrs down the phone. "Can you come around? I think I'm ready to sign the papers," she asks.

I should think twice about this, but I don't. "About fucking time, I'll be there soon." Hanging up the phone, I tell Blake what I'm doing before taking off from them.

Pulling up to her house, I can hear her crazy rat looking dog going nuts; the fucking thing hates my bike. The door swings open to reveal Bianca, dressed in a tight little get up. I instantly know her intentions, *obviously* and start walking back to my bike.

"Wait, Zane, I really am serious."

I spin around and glare at her. "Don't waste my fucking time Bianca, I'm not fucking interested in anything with you anymore, got it?"

I see her give up all hope in front of me, right before two life-changing words come out of her filthy mouth.

"I'm pregnant."

CHAPTER 7

ALAINA

I wake with not an ounce of a hangover, which is surprising considering how drunk I was last night. Looking at the time, I see it's eight in the morning, so I get up and call my tutors to let them know I won't be in for a couple of weeks, hoping that's enough time.

After calling school, I put on some running gear. I need a run to get my blood pumping. Pulling on some little black spandex shorts, and my fluro green sports bra, I pull my hair in a tidy ponytail before heading out the door.

Walking down the hallway, I see Ade coming out of a room. He stops in his tracks, eying my body. "Damn, little K, maybe you should have taken off some clothes last night," he teases.

I shove him in the shoulder and laugh. "Do you live here?"

He looks at his room, then back to me. "Nah, no way, Zane just has all of us staying here on lockdown until this shit with you blows over."

He sure is thorough, all though I wonder where *he* is. "Don't you guys have jobs or something?"

He laughs. "Yeah, just not the nine to five type." *Pack of mystery men.* His eyes go serious for a brief second. "Something tells me, if Zane sees you dressed like that, you're in trouble."

I roll my eyes at him. "I'm fine, Ade, I'm going for a run."

He looks down at my boobs that seem to be splashing out on display, thanks to my tight bra. "Yeah, not on your own you're not. Give me a sec and we can run together."

I agree, while waving my hand out, getting him to hurry up. I love spending time with Ade.

He walks out three minutes later, in basketball shorts, a shirt that has the Sinful Souls MC logo on it, and a flat baseball cap flipped backwards. I sigh inwardly at his sex appeal.

We head out onto the footpath past the gates and set off into a jog. "How was your sleep? That vodka knock you on your ass?" he asks with a smile.

I laugh. "Well actually, I feel fine. My ass is intact, thank you for your concern though. Have you seen Zane?" I ask him as we pick up our pace.

"He didn't come back last night," he replies in a clipped tone.

I stop jogging. "Oh ok, so let me get this straight. I meet him one night, and find myself exploring all kinds of naughty activities that I want to try with him. He also gives me the impression that he is interested too. Then I meet him a second time, he fucks me senseless, right before telling me that he set my friend up with Blake, just to get to me." I take a breath, before I continue. "Then, he leaves me at a clubhouse full of men, who I don't know by the way, while he's out, doing fuck knows what, with fuck knows who. I'm not cool with that."

He laughs, gripping his stomach, while still looking shocked. "Feel better after that little outburst?"

I smile back at him because I do feel better. "Much thank you. You know, when I met him, I thought it was by chance, and I thought we had some kind of connection. I guess it's stupid, he was pretty convincing though; in my defence." I look away, hiding my blush from the embarrassing realisation that he didn't actually want me.

He closes the distance between us before throwing his arm around my shoulder. "It's not stupid Alaina, you're fucking amazing, and don't forget that." He gives me a bump with his hip before setting off, leaving me to chase after him.

We round the corner to the clubhouse laughing, both hot and sweaty, when I notice a very pissed off Zane walking up to us. "Hello, Mr Biker, how nice of you to check in," I say with a sarcastic tone but don't stop jogging.

"Don't give me that fucking lip, Alaina." His fingers bite into my arm as he pulls me to a grinding halt. "What the fuck do you think you're doing walking around dressed like that? And what the fuck is this I hear about you on that stage!" I go to open my mouth but he shuts me down. "And *you,*" he spits at Ade. "I fucking said she's off limits. After hearing about you two playing around last night, I have to find you out here this morning." It's in that moment that I decide I've heard enough of his dominant, alpha male bullshit.

I yank my arm free of his grip and raise a finger to his face. "Excuse me, but the last I checked, I was a free woman, and a single one at that. I can dress, dance, and run with whomever I please." I stab my finger into his chest. "You do not get to fuck me senseless, before telling me it was all a part of some mysterious plan. Then leave me in a clubhouse full of men that I don't even know, while you fuck off for the night without so much as a second glance! So YOU can go fuck yourself Zane. I'm done with your games." I take a deep breath and storm off.

I see Felix stop him from chasing me in the corner of my eye, before I hear him say, "Sort your wife shit out first Zane."

The announcement stops me in my tracks. He has a wife. I knew it. I just knew something was off. His gaze locks on mine as I shake my head. I am so done with going along with his shit.

Walking into my room, I pull out my phone and ring Vicky, and she picks up on the second ring. *God, I've missed this voice.*

"Lainy!" I am hoping this good mood that she is in, will stick all through tonight, I need to get messy.

"I need to get drunk, and get beautiful. Or at least attempt it, and I need to be felt up by some sexy hot stranger," she giggles and it is like a light in my tunnel of darkness.

"Well, as far as greetings go, I think that one's my favourite. I'll come pick you up now?" just what I want to hear. "Thank you! I could kiss you right now" I reply, in a total non-lesbian, but maybe lesbian way. "I might take you up on that, see you soon."

I grab my wallet and phone, before heading downstairs. Just as I'm walking past the bar, I hear Zane mumble, "And where are you going?"

I turn around, finding him with his elbows resting on his knees, looking at me; but looking very deep in thought too. "Vicky's coming to get me, we're going out tonight. Girl's night. Don't worry, I'll be back around three in the morning, provided, I'm not under someone instead." I spin back around and proceed to head towards the door when he pulls me a stop by the arm. I'm thinking he must have spidey powers, he moved so fast from the sofa. Just as I think he's about to say something else, he lets me go.

"Just what I thought. I know what *I* want Zane, don't play with my emotions until you're sure of yours." He looks at me, eyebrows drawn in, with complete silence surrounding us. "Bye Zane," I scoff while continuing to walk toward my one night of freedom.

"Alaina," he says softly.

I turn around, hoping in some dreamland he would say some romantic shit about not wanting me to leave before sweeping me into his arms, while we kiss in the sunset. *I can pretend to like that sort of stuff.* However, this is not a fairy tale. My prince charming does not come riding a horse, he comes riding a Harley. He gives me a cold steady look. "You're taking a prospect with you." And with that, he leaves.

I stomp out like a toddler having a tantrum—immature I know. *Fucking men.* I pick Hunter; he's the cuter one, so he will be easiest to boss around. "Come on, pretty boy. You're on girls' night duty." His shoulders slump in defeat. "Fuck." He grabs his helmet, throws his leg over the bike, and waits for us to pull out.

Once we are on the highway, Vicky looks at me. "You good?" she asks.

I nod my head, "Yeah I'll be fine, I'm just so confused. I miss my uncomplicated life."

She looks at me, and innocently replies, "But your uncomplicated life didn't include a drop dead sex on two wheels biker?"

I laugh at her before adding, "Drop dead sex on two wheels married biker."

She slams on the brakes, and moves to the shoulder on the side of road. "Holy fuck, Vicky. What the hell is wrong with you? One little incident and bum boy behind us will call it in."

She looks at me, and I think I see steam coming out of her ears. Vicky comes from the good life, both parents are from money, she's had everything growing up, being the only girl and having two brothers. But her parents divorced when she was a little girl, because her dad decided the younger the better. So Vicky's hate for cheating husband's, runs very, *very,* thick.

"That fucking piece of slimy shit. I don't care about those pretty green eyes, or those perfect dimples, or that hellish smirk. Homeboy is going down." Even though she is completely serious, I have to laugh at her choice of words. "You know I love you, right?"

She looks over to me, and her face softens. "I love you too, girl."

I shoot a quick glance behind us, to see Hunter throw his hands up and mouth. "What the fuck!" I blow him a kiss and we carry on.

Being back in our apartment gives me good pre-biker vibes. It puts my feet back on the same level again.

I head straight for the shower, spending a little more time than necessary in there, before coming back out to find something to wear. "Okay Vick, I want a 'come get it' mixed with 'but will I give it?' outfit. Help me."

She looks over to me with a Cheshire cat smile and says, "I know just the piece."

***

We are currently up to five shots of tequila and three Cosmos into our night. It is safe to say, I'm feeling buzzed. Downing my drink in record time, I order more shots; because I really need to erase a certain biker off my brain, he is just one huge mind fuck.

"Oh my fucking god, who is that?" Hailey asks, looking over at Hunter.

"Oh, that?" I respond casually. "That's my babysitter, you like?" I ask, smirking and wiggling my eyebrows at her.

"Mmm, I like," as she heads over to him.

Hailey's cool, she is more Vicky's friend than mine, but she's always a good time.

I grab Vicky's arm and pull her to the dance floor. We start moving grinding and booty hopping all over the place, and it doesn't take long for guys to notice us; not that I think I'm the absolute best, but because Vicky's 'piece' she mentioned earlier was a ripper.

The white lace, skin tight, very short, long sleeve babydoll dress hugs my curves perfectly. I added my black over the knee-high stiletto boots, giving me a little edge, and I styled my hair in soft waves, while going heavy on the smokey eye. I added a little blush, and I was done. I don't wear foundation, I feel like it clogs my pores every time it's on my face. So with Vicky in her black and gold babydoll dress as well, we were sure to attract attention.

The two men who are coming up between us were cute enough, they are a little accountant looking for my liking; but the night was still young and we danced with them anyway. Until they got a little too touchy feely, then we decided to bail and get more drinks.

We down more shots, and it has me feeling a little dizzy now. Actually, I feel thoroughly wasted, borderline messy, which I don't do often at all, but the need to eliminate Zane from my brain was heading into desperate territory. I can't win, I need the distraction.

I go back on the dance floor, losing Vicky on the way. She seems to do that a lot lately.

I start to dance and lose myself in the music. My limbs feel loose when I feel hands take hold of my hips. I turn around and find a good looking guy matching my moves. *Impressive.* I smile seductively, *well at least I think it's seductive, I'm sure it definitely is not.*

He leans down. "What's your name?" I look up at him, and I notice how his stubble gives his baby face a nice darkness about him. I think I've found my distraction.

"Does it matter?" I ask.

He smirks before saying, "I guess not." He leans down, and attaches his lips to mine. It instantly makes me feel sick. All I want to do, is be in Zane's arms. Finding myself thinking about Zane again, I try to get greedy for more, more kissing, more touching. More attempts of getting

Zane out of my drunken mind, but it's not working. If anything, it's making me feel empty. I attempt project 'Forget Zane' once more, pulling my hand into mystery dancer's hair, and he groans into my mouth, pulling me right up into him, and causing me to feel the bulge between us. His lips on mine feel all wrong and his tongue dives into mine. *Uh, gross.*

He grabs my ass, and pulls me in closer. Just as I am about to push him away, he is already being ripped out of my hands. My brain takes a few seconds to catch up as I look at the absolutely livid biker standing before me.

CHAPTER 8

All I see is Zane throwing punches, I turn to see Blake and Ade next to him with humorous grins on their face. *Seriously! Fucking bikers.*

"Zane, what the fuck are you doing!" I scream.

He stops the pounding and spins around to face me. All I see is pure darkness in those eyes. "Me?" he roars. "More like what the fuck are you doing Alaina. Get outside now!"

I am way to drunk for this shit. "No, I'm not going anywhere with you, run back to your wife and leave the singles alone." I turn my back on him, about to storm off, when the next thing I know, I am upside down and staring at a sexy tight behind. He slaps my ass, and continues to walk out of the bar.

"Zane, put me the fuck down! Now!" My throat is instantly hoarse from screaming at him.

This is so embarrassing. "Zane! Everyone is staring at us." I watch a blur of faces whiz past me. "Why are you people not helping? What if I was really in trouble?" I ask, looking down the line of people.

I hear a group of older women look approvingly at him. "Giiirrlll, he can kidnap me, any day."

Just great. "Dumb cock thirsty females," I mumble to myself.

I hear Ade's chuckle following behind us, I can't see him, but I respond anyway. "Oh you think this is funny? You just wait Ade; you're on my shit-list too."

Zane puts me down, and looks at me. "What the fuck was that about, Alaina? Are you purposely acting like a slut, or are you always like this?"

I laugh at his audacity. "You're one to talk about being a slut, Zane! YOU'RE MARRIED!"

He looks at me, throwing his head back, and laughs. "That's what this is about? Because I'm married? I'm a grown man Alaina, I can fuck who I want. You wanted it. Looking at me all, 'Fuck me Zane, put your dick in my mouth!'"

Even in my drunk state, his comments sting. He wants to have his say, well so do I and I don't care how forthcoming I am. At least if he knows where I stand, and how I feel, then I know I've done my part. "Yeah, it is Zane. Because I actually thought we had a connection, stupid hey? Because not only are you married, but you're the president of a motorcycle club. I'm the dumbest bitch on the planet to think I could have had a chance with that, so yes *Zane*, you win. Yes I had feelings for you, but they all evaporated once I found out you had a *wife*."

He walks up to me, jaw clenched. "You don't know shit about my piece of shit marriage, maybe you should have asked me before making accusations, Alaina. I don't play fucking games." I look up to him, which is a long way up from my five foot six to his six foot two.

"And what would you had said? If I had asked you about your marriage, what would you had said?"

He closes his eyes before opening them again, clenching his jaw. "I would have said that she was the mistake I made after a night in Vegas, and I've been trying to divorce her since." His tone softens. "She was a mistake Alaina. Now I have to wait for two fucking years, because she won't sign the damn papers. She lives in her own apartment downtown. But you were right about one thing," he says, pulling me into him and brushing a few stray pieces of hair out of my very drunk face. "We do have a connection. I haven't been able to get you off my damn mind since the first night I met you, you're all I think about when I open my eyes and you're in my dreams when I close them." He pauses and so does my heart. "I'm fucking confused about these feelings because I've never had them before, ever. This isn't me Alaina, I don't do all that love shit." He lets out a breath and I relax a little, knowing I wasn't just imagining our attraction.

"I don't know what to say," I reply. He was always so cold and distant, and the times that I thought I did see some sort of emotion from him, I thought I must have imagined it. "I'm sorry, Zane."

He walks up to me, wrapping his hand around the back of my neck, caressing it lightly before kissing me like his life depends on it. The world can swallow us completely, and I would be one hundred percent in my happy place. Zane Mathews is my new happy place.

We come out for a breather, and he looks deep into my eyes. "Seeing him kiss you, was the worst thing I've ever had to fucking see, and I've seen some shit. But that, fuck. I wanted to kill him, I can fucking kill him!" he gets a little louder towards the end.

I look at him, bringing my hands to his face. "Don't." He instantly calms and grabs my helmet. I put it on, and feel the bike roar to life underneath me as we ride onto the highway.

Amo Jones

I'm having slightly paranoid thoughts, wondering if maybe I was too drunk to be riding; which made me hold on to him a little too tightly, all the way back to the clubhouse.

I get off the bike, with him pulling me in for another kiss, and then pushing his forehead up against mine for a brief second. "Come on."

Walking in this time, I get a few snarky stares from the club whores, which probably has a lot to do with the protective hand draped over my shoulder. Aside from that, we're greeted by cheering men, and with a few of them looking relieved. I hear a few mumble 'Finally' before he takes me up to his room.

His room is exactly like mine, there is nothing much to it. "Do you live here?" I ask him out of curiosity.

"Only when important daughters need protection," he answers with a smile. "No Alaina, I don't. I own a four bedroom house downtown, I go between the two."

I look at him, and there is so much I want to ask. I know that, now that we have the whole marriage issue out of the way, it is easier. But we still have a lot of hurdles that we are going to have to jump over; and I still don't know what this is.

"Sounds nice," I reply.

He comes up to me, picking me up, and wrapping my legs around him, as he throws me onto the bed. "I'm a lot of things babe, but *nice* is not one of them."

He crawls up my body, and props himself up onto his elbows. While looking down my eyes like I'm the most beautiful person he's ever seen. Obviously, I know this isn't true, but it's what his eyes are telling me. "Fuck your perfect," he whispers, making me nervous laugh, because I seriously think there should be different categories for laughs.

"Nowhere near," I reply, still blushing at his words.

He kisses me softly, so softly it makes my stomach ache and my skin burn. He slowly and passionately caresses my tongue with his, pushing one of my legs open with his leg, so he's resting right into my groin, all while never breaking the perfect rhythm of his kiss.

A little moan slips my lips, as he grinds himself into my body, while I instinctively push back. He runs his hands up my boots, slipping them under my dress, and pulling my G-string down. "Keep the boots on, fuck you look like you just stepped out of my perfect wet dream."

He pulls my dress over my head, and as much as I wanted this part to be glamorous like it is in the movies, it was not. My hair was everywhere, and my dress was so tight, that it took all my strength to pull it off my face; by the end of it, we were both laughing. God I love his laugh, it reminds me of how carefree he can be when it is just us and he is not carrying the world on his shoulders.

"Come here, baby," he says, smiling a full-blown dimple smile at me. He grasps onto my legs, and drags me down the bed, while pulling off his shirt.

I have to stare, because *damn,* that is a sight to see. His hair all messy, green hooded eyes with his dark lashes. He's too perfect for words.

He licks his bottom lip, and I see his lip ring jolt as he takes me in. I feel like he's fucking me with his eyes alone. Pulling my bra off, he gently sucks both of my nipples, as he lowers his beautiful face down to the apex of my thighs. I cry out in pleasure as he licks me softly, teasing my clit, giving it its own personal attention. "Fuck you taste perfectly sweet," he mumbles against me. I throw my head back as he opens up my folds, dipping his tongue inside, before making his way back to my clit. He pushes two fingers in, putting pressure on that perfect spot. He knows my body perfectly already. I lock up and I let my orgasm shatter through me. Looking down to him, I see him licking the evidence off his fingers with a lazy grin. "My favourite flavour."

He begins to take his belt off, pulling his jeans down as his cock springs free. My face lights up like Christmas. He crawls back over to where I am, and pushes into me. I cry out again as he fills me, inch by inch, pushing me to my limit. He starts kissing and sucking my neck, before he begins to move in and out. Starting out a slow, torturous, pace, before picking it up and pounding into me. It is not long before we are both getting lost in each other so deep, that I do not ever want to come back up.

He's lying on top of me, laying quick kisses on my lips, before pulling out of me. He slides behind me, pulling me in to spoon. I can barely keep my eyes open, while he is laying sweet little kisses on the back of my head. "Night, Zane," I say, drifting off to sleep. He squeezes me softly. "Night, baby." And for the first time in fifteen years, I feel protected.

CHAPTER 9

ZANE

Having her in my bed feels right, I don't give a fuck what anyone says, she's mine. Seeing her tonight looking sexy as fuck in that white dress, and my dick went hard the instant I saw her. That is until I saw the dead man walking, groping her ass, and sucking her face; then all I saw was red. If there wasn't a crowd, I would have shot him dead on the spot, and not thought twice about it. I'm not fighting my feelings for this girl anymore, I want her and only her.

Seeing Bianca here trying to pull the pregnancy card on me, didn't go down well. I told her that first of all, I don't believe a fucking word she's saying, and second of all, providing she is in fact pregnant; once she has had the baby, we would do a paternity test, and then, and only then, would I be involved. And I would be one hundred percent involved if it is mine. I may hate her, but I'll love the shit out of my kid, but until that day comes, I don't want to hear it.

I'm woken by a knock on the door. I normally wake up if someone so much as breathed on my face, that's how much of a light sleeper I am.

I pull on my jeans, and swing open the door. "What?"

Ade is standing there with a blank look on his face. "You got a problem."

I walk downstairs, and see the current problem. Why this bitch doesn't get it, is beyond me. I pull my shirt over my head, not missing the hungry look she's throwing my way. Bianca is hot, in the plain way that you find most girls walking down the street. Not Alaina though, she is unique, and not only is she beautiful and sexy, but she has that sassy mouth and is not afraid to tell me to get fucked if need be. I love that about her.

"What the fuck are you doing here, Bianca?" She gives Ade a look, and he gives her a disgusted one back. They never have liked each other, truth is, Ade never likes anyone. Until Alaina came along, Abby was the only girl he genuinely cared for.

"I wanted to show you a picture of the scan, look." I look down at her hands and see what she's holding. Inspecting the picture, it looks like a bean, but that's not what I'm really looking for. I'm looking for her name on the photo, and I see it. Her full name, date of birth, and address is also printed clearly on it. I still have my doubts, and I always will until the paternity test is done, because I know for a fact, that even though we messed around the most, she had another man on the side. I did not give a fuck about him. The bitch was just a convenience in the most inconvenient circumstances.

"Is this supposed to be you proving that you are pregnant?" I ask, looking at her with a bored expression.

"Yes Zane, and I am."

I laugh, giving the picture back to her. "It's not you being pregnant that I doubt Bianca. It's the fact that it's mine." Her eyes turn sad, obviously hoping that I'd give a fuck—too bad I don't.

"It's yours Zane, me and Jason stopped seeing each other the day he decided he wanted his family back." I laugh because it's the line most girls use.

"Yeah we'll see, in nine months."

She coughs. "Well actually, it's five months." I pause for a second while I do the calculations in my head, and the bitch is right, we fucked a lot around that time.

I look down at her stomach, and notice a tiny bump that you can hardly see, unless you knew how flat her stomach was before.

"My mind hasn't changed, I will only be involved once you've taken that test." She's just about to say something, when she stops and looks up the stairs. I see her face set into an understanding. Turning around, I see my girl walk down the stairs, and she stops to do a full body sweep of Bianca, then turns to look at me, like she's not worried. That's my girl; always on top of her game. That's exactly why I intend to make her my old lady.

CHAPTER 10

ALAINA

I wake to an empty bed, so I take this as my cue to get in the shower and wash away my morning breath, panda eyes, and tame this crazy hair. The warm shower welcomes me, using some cheap soap that they had in here already, but I instantly feel refreshed; making a mental note to buy some body wash and shampoo, because I have no idea how long I'll be here for.

I step out of the shower, and walk back into my room to find Vick on my bed.

"Holy shit, Vick!" Throwing my hands up to my chest.

She looks at me. "I need to tell you something, and it's not good, at all. And I don't know what to do." I walk over to her, clutching my towel.

"Okay, I'm listening." She looks up to meet my eyes, and it is then I notice she has been crying.

"I'm pregnant, Lain! Fucking preggers!" she almost yells throwing her hands up in the air. *Holy sweet fuck.*

"What! Are you sure? When did you find out?" I ask, as I sat down next to her on the bed in shock.

"Just this morning, I've been feeling a little sick lately, and I think I knew deep down that something wasn't right. But I was in denial, you know." Come to think about it, I don't remember her drinking last night.

"You disappeared last night, right before Zane went all, *me Tarzan, you Jane* on me."

She nods her head. "I know, I noticed them come in. I was trying to run away from them. I'm sorry Lain, I tried to get your attention, but you were on project 'be-a-whore' so I couldn't get your attention. I'm so sorry. I'm a horrible friend for just ditching." The fact that she was worried about what I would think from her ditching, tells you a lot about the type of friend she is.

"Seriously, it's fine. Don't worry about that, I can't believe this shit. And it's Blake's? Not Jesse's or anything?"

She looks at me, "Yes it's Blake's. I haven't touched Jesse in months. Since before spring break. Fuck, Alaina, Blake and I haven't spoken to each other in two weeks. Since I found out he was using me."

Oh crap! I forgot about that. "Oh fuck, I'm so sorry, I forgot all about that. There's just been too much going on." I begin to ramble, but she cuts in. "Lain, you have so much drama, it's fine, you didn't do anything wrong." I have no idea what she is going to do, all I know is I will be there for her to support her in whatever she needs.

"What are you going to do? I will support you whatever you decide to do, you know that right?" I say to her and she smiles, "I know, I better get going though. How was the rest of your night?" she asks with a light smile.

"It was...surprising" I reply, going red.

She laughs as she heads out the door, but then comes back in. "Please don't say anything to Zane yet, I haven't told Blake, and I don't know what I'm going to do yet. I might just head to the ranch for a bit, and turn my phone off until I figure it out. If you need me, call the ranch home line."

"Of course Vick, I love you."

"I love you too."

Once she's gone, I think again how fast our lives are changing with these bikers.

I start to head downstairs, hoping to find one of the prospects so he can take me to the supermarket. As I am coming downstairs, I see

Zane talking to a woman. Spotting me, she stops talking, and drags her eyes over me. I can tell by the way she's looking at me, that I've just met the Vegas mistake, so I ignore her, and look to Zane.

"Hey, I was just heading out to the supermarket. I can take Hunter with me if you're busy?" And before Zane can reply, she butts in.

"I'm Bianca, and who are you?" of course she has to be stunning.

I simply reply, "Alaina."

Zane grabs my hand, and pulls me to the side. I glance over to her, and she is smirking a nasty grin at me. "Take Hunter, I've got to sort this out," Zane replies. Looks like his wall has come back up.

"And what exactly is 'this'? Your wife?" I ask. I see his jaw ticking, and I know I have pissed him off.

"Yes, I can't get into this right now, I'll see you later."

Then he turns his back on me, walking away with his wife. The last thing I see before they round the corner, is her trying to take his hand. "Right then," I mumble to myself, as I head off to find Hunter. I feel like grinding him for info.

I walk over to Hunter, who is sitting on the picnic table with Harvey, Ade, Blake, and a prospect.

"Hey boys," I smile, pushing Blake over a bit so I can squeeze in. "What's everyone doing?" they all look at me with uneasiness on their face, except Blake and Ade, who both have a cheesy grin on theirs.

"Hey, sweetheart," as they both greet me with a kiss on the cheek.

"Blake, you're still on my shit-list with the number you worked on my best friend."

He drops his smile. "I'm sorry, Lain." He looks genuinely hurt, which is interesting, so I decide to lay off him, for now.

"Why is Zane's wife here?" I ask, just coming right out and saying it.

"I don't know, she never comes here. My guess is, she found out about you and came to size you up," Blake replies, taking a drink out of his beer.

I look over to Ade, who is sitting on my left side. I notice a couple of worry lines around his eyes. "Why do I feel like the slutty home-wrecker, Ade?" I almost whisper, trying to get any emotion out of my voice.

He puts his arm around my shoulder, and squeezes me into him, laying a kiss on my forehead. It's a sweet gesture, at least if things turn to shit for me and Zane, I may just have a friend for life with Ade—one could only hope anyway. "You're not Lain, you're amazing, remember? If Zane fucks up, my offer still stands," he responds with his carefree smile.

"You know, big boy, I think I might just love you," I say, smiling at my own words.

He whips his head around and looks at me. "Oh yeah?" Arching a proud eyebrow. "I think the feeling might be mutual." We both start laughing, and it feels good. I love that he always makes me laugh, as attractive as he is, and my god the man is beautiful. It's not like that with him and I, a little harmless flirting, yes, but under it all, we share a special kind of bond, the one you find once in a lifetime.

I almost forgot why I was here. "Hunter, can you take me to the store? I know I'm the only women here and everything, but there needs to be shampoo, soap, and a women needs tampons you know," I say tampons a little loud just to embarrass him.

His face pales. "Um, yes, okay, yep let's go," he replies awkwardly, scratching his head and not knowing where to look.

I glance back to Ade and Blake, catching them both laughing. "You evil, evil woman."

I smile and jump into the Escalade.

Once we are on the road, I look over to Hunter and he looks as uncomfortable as ever.

"Why do I make you uncomfortable?" I ask. I've always been a go-getter, I've never seen the point of beating around the bush; why waste your time asking yourself questions that you will never get the answer for.

"It's not that you make me uncomfortable," he replied, looking at me every couple of seconds. "It's that we have orders to protect you." He pauses briefly before adding, "And the last time one of us looked at you too long, they ended up head to head in the ring with Zane, and trust me, I do like my life."

I think over what he just said, ignoring the Zane comment. "Okay, do you know much about my dad?" I ask.

He looks at me again. "You trying to get me killed?" he questions with a smirk.

"No, not at all, I'm sure I'll get my answers soon enough."

We pull into the supermarket, and both get out of the car. He stops behind me, "I'll wait here while you go in and do your thing," he says, waving his finger towards the supermarket, with his other hand covering his mouth.

I laugh at him while walking towards the store. "Tampons, Hunter. They're just tampons." I glance over my shoulder to see him cringing, actually cringing for goodness sake. This man is prospecting for a notorious motorcycle club, and he is scared of tampons? Yeah, good luck with that.

My mindless thinking obviously distracts me, because when I turn my head back around, a black van pulls up next to me, with three men wearing black balaclavas slide the van door open and rush toward me. Big arms squeeze around my waist, cutting off any air circulation. Using the last of the breath I had, I scream, "Hunter!" And as if on cue, Hunter comes barrelling into us, pushing the man who had me around the waist over. He swings his right arm around, his fist connecting with one of the other men in the cheek. I hear a crack before the other two men round Hunter and all start pounding into him until eventually he falls to the ground. "Alaina!" the urgency in Hunter's scream jolts my body to life bringing a rush of panic. I turn on my heel, ready to run when one of them gets me in a sleeper hold while holding a rag over my mouth before everything goes black with the last thing on my mind being—tampons

CHAPTER 11

ZANE

Walking away from Alaina right now is what's best. I will explain everything to her when the time is right. I feel Bianca trying to latch onto my hand, and I quickly pull it out of her grasp. "What the fuck do you think you're doing?" I ask, and she turns red. "I miss you, I miss us."

"You're delusional. There was no us, you were looking for a good time, and you found it, quit the fucking around."

She jumps into her car. "I'll see you in five months, daddy." She revs the engine and skids out of the compound.

"Crazy fucking bitch."

I look over to the picnic table, and see Alaina sitting, laughing with the brothers. Although it fucks me off initially, it also makes me realise how easily she has fit in here. No one fits in here, especially females. She seems to be smart enough to know her position, and when not to push. She can push all she wants with me, but my club is separate, and is no place for a woman; especially one as gorgeous as Alaina fucking Vance, even if all these fuckers have fallen for her.

I watch her as she gets up, and starts walking to the Escalade with Hunter. I know I could probably go with her, but I need to make a call to have Bianca followed. She has to be playing me.

I hang up the phone with one of our prospects, when it immediately begins to ring again. I pick it up instantly when I see that it is Hunter.

"Fuck Zane, I'm sorry, I fucked up, I fucked up, FUUUCCKK!" is all I hear from the other end of the phone. Knowing it's Hunter and knowing that Alaina is with him, I jump out of my seat.

"What? What the fuck is going on."

"She was walking into the store, she was right there, I was fucking talking to her. Then this black van pulls up, a couple of men in suits and balaclavas jump out, one takes hold of her and I run in there swinging, I got a few hits in before they all took me down. Fuck I'm so sorry, Zane. "

I feel emotionless, with nothing but murder and complete utter rage pulsing through my veins.

"Where are you?" I ask, in a shallow low voice.

After getting my answer, I walk out the door, and slam it shut behind me, before looking up to the sky. I want to scream bloody murder.

Making my way to my bike, all I see is red, red for blood, because I am fucking blood thirsty.

"Z?" Ade and Blake come up to me, sensing something is wrong.

"Z, hold up!" Ade yells, catching up to me.

I spin around, not knowing how to piece the words together, but managing to spit out, "Alaina's been taken."

I see both Ade, and Blake stiffen while they grow angry. Ade's face turns frantic, before he runs to his bike. I get on mine, and we speed all the way to the store.

Pulling up, I see the Escalade. Throwing my helmet to the ground, I make my way towards Hunter; ready to slit his fucking throat, right here in this car park.

Felix comes up behind me, taking my arm. "I know you're mad brother, I know you're looking for an out right now, but don't do it. He tried, Zane, he fucking tried. He did was he was supposed to do – but three on one – even you know is not a fair fight. Hunter is valuable, the best prospect we have. As much as all of us want to kick his ass right now, we need to concentrate on getting your girl back. He can be punished when she's back safe in your arms."

The fucker makes sense, but I carry on towards him anyway, I open the driver's side door, and give him a swift punch to the jaw. "You're fucking lucky that's all you're getting." He rubs his jaw, looking at me with red pained eyes.

"Where the fuck were you, and why were you not with her!" I yell at him.

"I'm sorry Zane. She was just running in and out, I thought she would be fine; I fucking, tried. I...fuck." He has tears coming down his face, giving me enough satisfaction for now.

I turn, and walk towards the store, heading straight to the office and demanding for the last footage they would have. The manager agrees, showing me clearly what had happened. I write down a copy of the plates. While we continue to watch the video, it makes me sick to my stomach. When I see the part where they take her, I lose my shit, and lay my fist into the closest wall. "FUUUCCCKKK!" I roar, breathing heavily.

Blake puts his hand on my shoulder. "We'll find her brother, no matter what. We will find her."

CHAPTER 12

ALAINA

The first thing I can taste is blood. The second thing is the smell of blood, and the third thing I know, due to my blocked ears, the unsteadiness of the floor, and the light sound of jet engines, is I'm on a plane.

I try to open my eyes, but it takes a couple of times because one of them is swollen shut, while the other has dry blood around it. I pull on my hands, which are tied to the roof, and my feet are tied together as well, no luck there.

I try to focus my eyes, then I see someone come out of the shadows. My breath catches in shock when I see that it's the guy I was dancing and sharing spit with at the club. "Where am I?" I croak out.

He laughs, "Hell." He punches me again, right in the face, knocking me out in one hit.

⌇ ⌁

The next time I open my eyes, I'm in a bedroom. It is a tiny room, but aside from that, it has a modern, cottage style to it. It has huge high ceilings, and a bed which sits right in the middle of the room.

I try to pull on my arms and legs, with no effect, probably because I am tied to rings, which are built into the floor. I start to panic when I realise I can't get free.

The door flies open, revealing the guy from the nightclub; who walks directly to me, and unlocks me from the rings; but replaces them with handcuffs. "If you try to run, Barbie, I'll cut your tits off." How did I not see this obvious psychopathic human being when I was so eager to open my legs for the fucker? Looks like I have a tendency to attract the psychos too, *just bloody great*. He looks at me. "Are you not going to ask where you are?"

"I know enough. Wherever I am, I know Shane Amaro is in the same building," I respond.

He chuckles before saying, "Smart girl, for a blonde."

He pulls at my handcuffs and starts dragging me down the hallway. The more I really look at the place, I notice that all the rooms are in a line. There has to be over twenty rooms just on this one level, and something tells me, there are different levels in this huge old mansion.

We get into the elevator, and he pushes six – six – six into the control panel. I scoff, "How fitting." Dancer man turns his head around to me. "Fuck up, you don't speak." I roll my eyes, because I know that Shane is not going to kill me, if he wanted to, he would have done it by now; also, how is he supposed to get his pay back if I am dead?

The elevator doors ping, opening right out into a huge, circle, wrap around lounge, with glass floor to ceiling walls that go all the way around. Obviously so he can have a panoramic view of the entire property.

There's a man standing still right in the middle, looking over his empire. I wait for him to turn, and when he does, it's like looking into the eyes of the devil in flesh. An evil, old, wrinkled, gold toothed grin spreads out on his face.

"Hello Alaina, welcome back to New Zealand."
Oh fuck.

CHAPTER 13

ZANE

I'm sitting at the head of our table, when a call comes through. After seeing it's Joseph, I answer straight away. "They got her," I say, and the line goes quiet for a few brief seconds.

"What do you mean, they got her," he asked in a flat tone.

"She took one of the prospects to the shop with her, while he was waiting in the car, they took her. He didn't go down without a fight though. I got the CCTV footage of the car, so I'm faxing them to you now."

More silence and I think the line has cut out. He coughs before saying, "I know exactly where she will be, it's too late."

What the fuck does he mean it is too late? "I will find her, not for you anymore, but for me," I respond.

"I wasn't meaning for you to give up, I'm going to have to find a way to get you and your club to New Zealand." Then the line goes dead. Fuck. Could she really be all the way on the other side of the world? I feel empty. I just had her in my arms less than forty eight hours ago.

Looking up, I see Ade staring at me with red bloodshot eyes. "We need to get her back brother," he says sadly.

"I fucking know that Ade, she is MY girl, remember that."

He nods, and leans back on his seat.

"That was Joseph, he's getting us over to New Zealand. He'll call us back soon," I say, before I begin to make my way to the bar, snatching a bottle of whisky. I start guzzling it like it's water as I make my way to a spot, sitting down at one of the tables.

Movement by the door catches my attention and I see Blake walk in. "Not a good idea, Prez. You need to be on your game." I look up to him with my arms fisting on the table. "Is it Vicky that has just been kidnapped?" I asked, looking at him as if I want to rip his throat out.

He winces at the mention of her name, fucking knew it. I knew he was pussy whipped, the minute he laid eyes on her.

"I rest my case brother," I reply, continuing my drinking until my world goes black.

I can't fucking live without this girl.

I wake to the ringing of my phone. "What!" I answered, scrunching my eyes from the early morning sun blaring into my room.

"Got your way in."

I shoot up, throwing my jeans on, despite my pounding headache.

After explaining where we need to go, I run downstairs.

"Everyone in the boardroom, now!"

Sitting at the end of the table, I look over the men that are willing to lay their lives down. The praise can come after I get my girl home safe.

"Joseph has called me this morning to tell me he has our way in; we will be flying by private jet, courtesy to the Confederation of Assassins. It turns out, they only care once shit gets real." I rub one hand down my face, "If you're out, say so now. It's a lot to ask and I get that." I look around at them, while they all express their one hundred percent commitment to getting her back.

"I appreciate this boys, but if shit goes sour, I'll need a solid crew back home." I stand from my seat before saying, "We should only be a week at the most, and I'll let you know if we will be gone longer."

I begin walking back upstairs to gather my shit, I feel like I'm on autopilot; the need to have her back is at an all-time high.

Out of everyone, I end up with Blake, Ade, Felix and Ollie. That is all the army I will need. "Follow me out." They all nod their head, while fastening their helmets, as we floor it at record time to the local private airport.

Pulling up at the gate I was told to ride to, I see Joseph getting out of his limo; looking like he has not aged at all.

"Bit flash don't you think?" I ask. He laughs while buttoning his suit jacket up. "Sorry I can't accommodate to your needs," he replies with a smile, before he continues. "We're leaving in twenty minutes. Your bikes will be there when we land." I don't ask questions, because I know very well how many connections Joseph has.

"We?" I ask him.

"Yes, we," he replies. "There's no one I love more than my daughter Zane, I won't rest until Amaro's blood is raining down on hell itself."

"That's a beautiful thought," I laugh and vow the same as we all start to board the private jet.

I see Blake on his phone. "Come on brother, we're not waiting on you."

He looks up to me, hanging up his phone. "Vick isn't answering her phone, I haven't been able to get through to her in weeks, she doesn't even know about Alaina."

Snatching his phone off him. "And that's a good thing, we don't need her flipping out, pushing herself onto this ride as well, because you know she will."

He nods his head in agreement. "Alright brother, let's get your girl back."

CHAPTER 14

ALAINA

He's walking towards me with a smug look on his face. He hasn't changed much, just his obvious aging. He stands slightly on the shorter side, with his grey hair slicked back; dressed in an immaculate grey suit and a gold chain around his neck, looking very much like what I see in my nightmares.

He runs the back of his hand down my cheek, and my body instantly flinches away. He chuckles before asking, "Do you know why you're here Alaina?" I do, I remember everything this sick pig told me.

"Yes, I have an idea why, you will need to enlighten me on the rest though." I work to keep my face stoic.

He points to the large couch that sits in the middle of the room. "Sit." Doing as I am told, I make my way to the sofa.

He begins to pour himself a drink, before coming to sit opposite me, placing the glass down with a loud clunk. He rolls up his sleeves, and props his leg on his knee. "What do you know about your father?" he asks as he collects his glass and takes a sip, his eyes never breaking from mine over the rim.

I look at him. "Only what any innocent eight year old girl would think of the only hero in her life."

He laughs and takes another sip. "Hero? No. Unless your hero is the CEO of the Confederation of Assassins."

I stop all of my thoughts. "What?" I ask in a whisper. I'm shocked, it can't be, this must be a lie. My dad was a loving man, he had everything to give for me and my mother, we were the center of his world.

I hear Shane laugh, and throw back the rest of his drink, before getting up to pour another. "Yes, and when you were to turn eight, you were to come with me to be groomed for my son. I believe you've met him;" he says with a wide grin. I see him curl his finger back. "Bring him in." I turn around to see the same men that carried me in, carrying a very bloody, and beaten Jesse.

They throw him down on the floor where he curls up in the fetal position. "JESSE!" I scream, as I get up to run to him.

He's struggling to breathe from coughing and looks almost dead. Tears start streaming down my cheeks, as I'm trying to do a quick check over his injuries. Most of the injuries on his face look worse than they actually are, but I don't know what's going on internally. My fingers press against his throat when he struggles to speak, "I'm sorry, Alaina. I tried to stall him off," he whispers. One of the men then kicks him right in the stomach.

"STOP!" I scream, trying to shield Jesse with my body. "How could you let this happen to your own son?"

"Easy, he betrayed me, those who betray me, get punished." He starts to walk over to where we are, and I pick up Jesse's head, laying it on my legs as I whisper, "Hang in there J, we're getting out of here, I promise."

A roar of laughter pierces my ears. "You think you can get out of here?" Shane asks me while still laughing.

"*I know* we'll be getting out of here."

He stops laughing, tilting his head to the side. "And what makes you think that I won't just you kill you now?"

"The fact that you just went through a great deal of trouble to get me here," I reply with venom in my tone. I close my eyes briefly, before opening them again. "Why do you want me here? Now that your first plan isn't happening?"

He kneels, looking me right in the eyes. "We'll see now, it's not you that I'm actually interested in." He responds with a smile, looking up at one of his men before looking back to me. "I knew that once I started tailing you, your father would know, because he's been keeping such a close eye on you all these years."

I take a second to try to piece together what he is telling me, he wants my dad? That is what this is about? "He's made himself non-existent, you don't find Joseph Vance, he finds you." He stands before continuing. "Do you want to know why you were to be mine on your eighth birthday?" he asks, before laughing and turning back around to me. It wouldn't matter if I said no, he was going to tell me.

"Let's start with your mother." He gulps his drink in one go. "Your mother was my wife, but your father fell in love with her, and apparently the feeling was mutual." He looks down on me briefly. "I could have killed them both, then and there, but I didn't, instead I made a deal with them. When she conceives, the child would be mine to groom, either for my son, or as a fighter if you were a boy. Do you know how powerful the Vance name is Alaina? People drop to their knees just at the thought of passing Joseph on the side of the street. Power equals more money, I wasn't completely sure what I was planning for you yet, but I knew I wanted you. I then found out that your mother couldn't have children, they had made that deal thinking I would never find out. The day she found out that she was with child, was the day I was going there to kill them both. My wife at the time was also carrying, a boy, while your mother was carrying you; well, you can only imagine my excitement, it was like fate. I told them I would return when you were eight to collect you." He says with a huge smile plastered on his face. I am in total shock but he carries on, "When he gets here, him and I are going to settle a very ancient score."

I'm squeezing Jesse, hoping that this is some sort of bad dream. "You're sick," I say disgusted by his speech only to be met with a grin.

"Thank you," he replies.

In his sick mind, he thinks that was a compliment. "Get them out of here," he spits in disgust.

The next thing I know, I am being pulled up from behind, along with Jesse. "Get up!" Dancer man shouts near my ear.

Standing to my feet, I help Jesse up, draping his arm over my shoulder so he can lean most of his weight on me. He sucks in a breath and clutches his ribs. They begin to pull us, so we start walking down the same way we came through. Once we reach a door, one of the men opens it, while the other shoves us in. Slamming the door behind us, I hear the lock slide across; locking us in. "Fuck," I say, as I pull Jesse across to the bed in the middle of the bedroom.

I look around the room, there is a desk on the opposite side of the bed, and a window opposite the door, but it is bolted in. I know straight away that our escape will not happen this way. I will have to figure something else out. Jesse gingerly sits on the bed and I help him lift his legs.

"Let me have a look at you," I say quietly while lifting his shirt. His torso's marred with blood, seeping wounds and heavy bruising. My fingertips cause him to flinch as I start at his collarbone and feel my way around. I don't dare touch the black purple bruise over his left rib cage. I gently help lift his arm and I stop immediately as he sucks in a breath.

"Sorry."

I place his arm back down. Far as I can tell broken ribs and all I can do is make him comfortable while I figure a way out.

"Do you feel dizzy? Did they get you in the head?"

"They got me everywhere," he struggles to say.

Taking hold of the sheet on the bed, I start cleaning the seeping wounds on Jesse's face. "Jesse? Talk to me, don't go to sleep okay?" I say softly.

He tilts his head to me, he's struggling to look at me with both eyes swollen shut. "I won't go out like this, baby girl, don't you worry." I kiss his forehead and lay next to him. "I'm so sorry Jesse, I'm sorry that's your father." And I watch him drift off into a deep sleep.

CHAPTER 15

ZANE

We have just landed at an airport in Auckland, New Zealand. Stepping out onto the tarmac, a shiver runs over my skin; its fucking cold and the air is crisp.

"The bikes are here, sir," Joseph's assistant says to him.

After he gets off the phone, we follow Joseph around to the back of a big building, lifting the garage doors we see all our bikes lined up inside.

"Follow us, we have a safe house here," Joseph says as he jumps into another limo. The man goes everywhere in style, and aside from the fact that he was the most infamous assassin that went down in history—worldwide. He loves his family. Putting on our helmets, we ride out.

The safe house is a huge stone house, surrounded by a fully fenced yard. Pulling up, I see all cameras surrounding the entire house.

"All this necessary?" I asked him. Cameras mean evidence, which makes that against what I want.

"Yes, Amaro will be expecting us; I have no doubt that this has been his plan all along." "What do you mean?" I ask, as we make our way into the house.

"I mean, he's wanted me here all along, but in all the years I tried, I could never track him down, until we bugged Alaina's necklace."

I fucking knew this was a fucked up idea. "So you mean to tell me, that you were counting on the fact that she would get taken?"

He looks at me, realising what I'm accusing him of. "Don't get mad on me now son, I love my daughter, and there is nothing I wouldn't do for her. It's why she has been safe all these years, but yes I was. It was our only chance. He's been ghost for fifteen years."

I want to rip out his black fucking heart. "You don't love her! You do not fucking gamble on someone you love, Joseph! Fuck! What the fuck am I here for then? If this was your genius plan all a fucking long?" I'm seething and to say that I'm fuming, would be a complete understatement.

"Why do you think I didn't kill him all those years ago, when she was a baby? The Confederation do not deal with personal issues, I have to deal with this and I stand alone. I knew you and your boys were the next best thing, so that is why you're here."

"So that big fucking jet is yours then; I don't fucking like being played, Joseph," I say with a steady glare.

"I was going to tell you, but the next time I spoke to you, I fucking heard it in your voice son, I heard the love you have for her. I couldn't risk you fucking up this plan." Although I'm absolutely foaming at the mouth with anger, I see his reasoning, because damn fucking right I would have stopped this shit from going down.

"Don't fucking do it again, I don't care what your current occupation, or reputation is, I'll slit your fucking throat in your sleep," I say with complete seriousness. He chuckles and nods. That nod was him showing a mutual understanding of business.

I walk through the front doors of the house, and it has a vintage, new style look to it. I hate it immediately; it reminds me of everything that Alaina is. I make my way to the lounge and notice all the sheets draped over the slightly out-dated furniture. Looking around the large area, I see a huge family portrait hanging up above the open fire.

"Was this your home?" I asked, feeling Joseph walk up behind me. "Back then, was it your house?" I repeat myself.

He passes me a glass of some strong amber liquid before replying, "Sure is."

My heart jolts in my chest; I need my fucking girl back now. "We need to work fast, we need to get her back now," I say to him. He nods his head while taking a gulp of his drink. "We are and we will, as soon as the sun goes down we will leave, but first, I want to show you something."

I follow him out of the lounge, through the huge opening glass doors that open out onto a patio and grass area. There are a couple of trees, and a large tree house in the backyard. I love that fucking tree house, picturing Alaina as an innocent child makes me want to settle down and have kids with her. She's my fucking world, and tonight, I'm going to raise hell to get her back.

We are walking across the grass area to what looks like a large garden shed; he opens the door and steps in. I look around and it is empty, apart from a large rug on the floor, Joseph pulls the rug over, revealing a trap door.

Opening it, we head down the steep stairs, he pulls on a string to turn the light on and I look around in amazement; seeing the walls covered with all the weaponry you can think of, from shotguns, to AK 47s, AR 15s, grenades and grenade launchers. My fingertips run over the ballistic vests and eye over the amount of ammunition. I pull a vest off the hanger and drape it over my torso, pulling the straps tight.

I drag my eyes away from the beauty in front of me, to meet his stare and smirk.

"Let's go get our girl back."

CHAPTER 16

ALAINA

I wake to find Jesse sitting up in the bed. Realization of where I am hits me and I sit bolt upright. Jesse puts his hand on my shoulder and I relax into his touch.

I rub my eyes. "Shit, how long have I been out?"

He smiles. "Not too long, a couple of hours at most."

Swinging my legs over the bed, I say, "We need to get out of here Jesse, I don't care who I need to kill, we need a plan." It's then that the windows rattle from a huge explosion coming from the front of the house.

"Holy fuck!" I run to the window, and see the front main gate go up in flames.

"Jesse, I think our escape just blew up the front gate," I look to him smiling.

"It's about fucking time," he replied under his breath, and just when I was about to ask what exactly he meant by that comment, I start to hear footsteps running towards our room.

I run to stand by Jesse, when our door swings open, with Mr Dancer and his men standing before me. "Get the fuck up, it's time."

We are being dragged down the long hallway, the guards have their guns raised. We quickly make it outside to where a large pool is, it is the first time I have actually seen the house, it's huge, mansion huge. If I had to guess, I would say twenty bedrooms and four floors.

Looking out to the farmland that surrounds us, I see people running around frantically, they look like normal people, until you look closer and notice they are all dressed in the same clothes; the majority of them are young.

"Jesse," I whisper next to him loudly. "What exactly does your father do?"

He looks angrily out at to field. "Slavery, people owe him money for gambling, or favours, so they pay with time spent here. They usually choose to." He looks out completely blank before continuing. "That's the adults, the children though?" he says with huge sadness and anger in his voice. "They're pulled out from all over the place for different jobs, mainly to train for underground fighting. The girls get sold out to rich capable buyers; I believe the correct term is —" I look out in front of me, my face turning pale and feeling sick to my stomach.

"Trafficking," I say to myself, more than to anyone else.

It's then that I decide I don't care if I go down. I will get these people out of here.

I see them all running to a big barn, and for a split second, I think I see my mother. Only older, skinnier, and ghost looking.

I didn't know I'd stopped walking, until I feel a rough shove from behind me. Noticing that that is the way we are heading, I ask, "Where are you taking us?" The man behind me shoves me again. "Fucking walk, before I knock you out cold and rape you in your sleep."

I scrunch my face up in disgust; to think people like this actually exist is scary. And as much as I will fight, I'm terrified of what's to come. A tear escapes down my face and I startle when three clear gunshots ring out. I wipe the blood off my face, the once tight grip that was around my arm, now gone. A crumpled bleeding body lays at my feet.

I turn to see Zane, dropping his arm back to his side. "Zane?" I scream, as I run up to him. Something happens when I am around him, I've spent all my life taking care of myself, being strong for myself, but around Zane, I know he can do it for me.

"Come here, baby," he reaches his arms out to me, and I go jumping into them. I kiss him as if it is the last kiss we will ever have.

"Um, I don't mean to interrupt this epic reunion, but we still have people that are trying to kill us," I hear Jesse say nervously.

Zane lands three single kisses on my lips before he puts me down, pushing me behind him. He looks straight at Jesse. "And what fucking part have you played in this whole thing?" he asks, as he begins to walk up to him.

It is then that I realise what Zane is implying, so I quickly run up in between the two. "Stop, Zane, it's not what you think. The reason he looks the way he does is because he went against his father's wishes."

Zane then snaps his head to Jesse. "Father?" he roars as he pulls his gun up to Jesse's forehead. "You're the motherfucker she was supposed to be with?"

"Zane, I swear to fucking god, if you don't stand the fuck down right now, I will never forgive you. You do not have to trust him, but you will trust me; he is on our side, now, put the fucking gun down. Now!"

He looks at me, then looks at Jesse. "Zane! Now!" I repeat, and as if on cue, he lowers the gun. "You're fucking lucky that I love this girl, and if I ever find out you crossed us? I will eighty-six you so fucking fast, you won't know what hit you. Are we fucking understood?"

He loves me? "You love me?" I asked shyly.

His eyes turn gentle instantly, "I fucking love you, baby." My eyes water again, as I wrap my hands around his neck. "I love you too, Zane Mathews."

I hear Jesse in the background again. "Guys? Seriously, we are sitting ducks out here. Alaina, only you would choose to declare your love in the middle of a war."

I giggle in between kisses, then Jesse adds, "For the record Zane, I have never wanted to hurt Alaina, ask her father, he will tell you." Zane nods, accepting his explanation for now. "Let's go."

He begins to lead us the opposite way of the barn, and towards the Hummer that's waiting for us at the gate. "Zane wait no, I want to get those people out," I say, panicking.

He does not stop walking. "We will, but not right now. Right now, I just want you safe."

I pull my arm out or his grasp. "No, I want them safe, now. And I want Shane dead."

He stops in his tracks, "Alaina, for once can you do as you're fucking told and just get in the fucking truck!" he yells in frustration.

I quickly snatch his second gun, that I know he always keeps in his holster on his jeans, and start running towards the barn. I know how to shoot, I have not shot anything in a long time, but I have memories of my father and I going hunting when I was a child. I'm no professional, but I know, I just know, that if I have to; I will kill to get these people safe.

I hear Zane yell from behind me, "ALAINA! FUCK," while he starts running up behind me.

I turn around to see Blake and Ade jumping out of the truck to chase me too, Zane catches up to me and pulls my arm into him. "Fucking stop! Joseph is in that house as we speak, with Ollie and Felix having a war of their own. I need to be in there with them, and you need to go back to the safe house; these people will be safe once Shane's dead!"

I look at him and say, "I think I saw my mother." Before turning around, and sprinting into the barn.

Looking to my right, I see a guard start to pull out his gun; before I realise what I'm doing, I point my gun right at him; then I pull the trigger without flinching, getting him right in the head.

Adrenalin surges through my body. I look around and see another man in the upstairs stables looking down on everyone. I point my gun at him, shooting again; right in the forehead. *Holy shit, I just killed two people.*

Gunshots ring out near me, so I duck behind a big box of hay until they stop. I stand and start shooting where the shots were coming from, snagging someone else in the process; watching him fall and land in the middle of the crowd of people.

I look to my left and see Zane, Blake and Ade standing there staring at me in awe. "What?" I asked them.

Ade looks like he has seen a ghost. "I would hug the fucking shit out of you right now. But you're going to need to give me some time to calm the *hoe wrecker* down, because holy fuck, I'm so turned on right now." I smirk at him and realise how fucking much I've missed this big beast of a man. I go running up to Ade, in full blast mode and jumping onto him. He starts laughing, "Hey, baby girl. I might start calling you firecracker after that performance." He smirks up at me. "You call your dick a 'hoe wrecker'?" I asked, in fits of laughter.

I feel large hands wrap around my waist, pulling me out of Ade's grip. Once my feet are set back on the ground, I look up to see Zane clenching his jaw together. "Fucking boundaries you two, fucking watch it." I roll my eyes. "You know I love you, Zane." He smiles his perfect smile at me like those are his new favourite words. He doesn't need to know that I said the "L" word to Ade first, he might end up shooting us all in this very spot.

"I know baby, but don't ever fucking do that again." I look to Ade and shrug at him. "I did miss you, big boy." His eyes twinkle, *actually fucking twinkle*. "I missed you too, firecracker."

I look over to Blake. "Hey Blake." He pulls me in for a hug, "Hey firecracker, that was pretty fucking impressive, how'd you learn to shoot like that?" I laugh and respond. "My Dad."

We are all laughing, when I hear a soft voice call out my name. "Alaina?" I turn to a voice from my past. The voice I have only heard in my dreams for the last fifteen years. The woman before me is my formerly beautiful mother looking frail, under fed, and pale; with dark circles under her eyes.

"Mom?" I whisper, wrapping my arms around myself. "Is it really you?" She starts walking up to me, until Zane steps in front of me, blocking her from my view.

I step around him, as she replies. "Yes sweetie, it's really me," tears pouring down her face.

I instantly run up to her and wrap her in my arms. "Oh Mom!" tears streak from my eyes as she places both hands on my face and looks deep into my eyes. "Oh baby, I'm so happy that you're okay." Her thumbs wipe away the tears.

It is then that my dad walks in through the doors. With Ollie, Felix and some other man I have never met on his tail. "Dad?" I whisper, as he comes running up to me, picking me up into his arms. "My baby girl," he mumbles into my hair as he holds me tight. Sobs rack through my body as I cry for all the years I've lost with my parents. I never thought I would ever see either of my parents again, so getting them both back is remarkable.

Looking down, I notice all the blood on his top. "Shane?" I asked and he puts me down, trying to find a way to sugar coat the truth.

Zane steps in. "Oh, you don't need to dress the truth pretty for your little princess over here, she just gunned down three men, shooting two of them right in the forehead."

My dad chuckles with pride in his eyes, "Got that impeccable aim. You may look like your mother, but at least you shoot like your daddy. It's a family gift that is passed down." He presses a kiss to my forehead.

He turns his attention to the crowd of people. "The police are on their way. Shane's dead, and you're all free." It feels like a huge weight has been lifted off my shoulders, I step aside so he can see my mother, and you know when he spots her because his whole face lights up.

"Jennifer?" he asks, and as he starts walking towards her, his shoulders shaking show that he's crying.

She smiles with her arms outstretched. "It's me, Joseph."

He picks her up, and kisses her so hard that I have to look away. When he puts her down, he looks over to us. "We have to go, now." Then he looks over to the one hundred or so people in the barn. "You have nothing to be scared of, you're all free."

I thought I would feel shit about taking not one, but three people's lives, but I don't because when I look around, I see what they were hiding and what they were supporting. But I see that there are children as young as ten in here. Fuck them, I'll shot them all over again in a heartbeat.

I see my dad pull my mom into his arms. "Let's go home."

CHAPTER 17

Pulling up to my family home, it brings back a swarm of memories. All happy ones, except that one day fifteen years ago.

Rounding the big circle garden at the front of the house, I have my head resting on Zane's shoulder, tired from everything that has happened. The car stops, and Zane pulls me into his arms, carrying me into the house and right up to my childhood bedroom.

Once we get inside, I look around. "Wow," I say in amazement, nothing has changed. My big, four-post Victorian bed is to the left of the room, sitting the same way I left it, with lace nets draping around the outside. I used to love that as a kid, it made me feel like I had my very own fort every time I went to bed.

Sitting on either side of that are my white bedside tables, with photos on each one. And opposite my bed is a large vintage set of drawers; with a large mirror sitting on top. My mom restored it when I was six, and I loved it instantly.

To the right of the drawers, is a door that opens up to my walk in closet. I step into it, turning the light on. I look behind me and see Zane taking off his entire armoury, without taking his eyes off me. Turning my attention back to the wardrobe, I touch all my tiny clothes. It is like taking a drive down memory lane, it feels surreal.

I walk out, heading towards the final door in my bedroom, on the other side of the drawers is the ensuite. I always loved the decor in here, with its baby pink and grey striped walls. I see the big spa bath sitting in the middle to the left of the room, with the bathroom sink and toilet in front of me. "Cute," Zane says, looking around the bathroom with a smile on his face. "Yeah, it is," I reply before turning around and walking up to him, grabbing his face between my hands, and kissing him softly on his perfect pouty lips. "I thought I'd never see you again," I whisper, looking into his eyes.

"As if I would ever let that happen baby, I plan to build a life with you, and nothing or nobody will ever be able to get in the way of that," he replies caressing my cheek.

I lean into his gentle touch and close my eyes. When I open them, I find him staring at me with such intensity it makes my skin burn while setting my soul on fire. "I'll run the bath, as much as I want to fuck you from now until next week, I want to take care of you first," he says and my face drops. I love having sex with Zane, it's my favourite thing to do and every time with him has been amazing. He makes me feel beautiful and untouchable.

"Okay then, I'll just grab some clothes." I walk out of the bathroom, only to spin around and walk back in to see him turning the taps on. "I don't have any clothes," I scoff.

He laughs. "Red bag on the floor, I packed some shit for you." He smiles his sexy smile at me, and I blush at his thoughtfulness.

"Thank you."

Walking back out, I get my pajamas with my tank top out of the bag. I have to smile; they will always remind me of our first encounter.

I head back into the bathroom and see Zane pour some lavender oil into the bath, when the sweet smell hits my nose, I close my eyes and inhale deeply, it brings back so many memories; I never thought I'd experience that smell while being in this bathroom ever again. The whole situation is so surreal.

Proceeding to strip down, I notice Zane glaring at my body with his jaw ticking, if he puts any more pressure down, I am sure he will break his teeth.

"What?" I ask him. Looking down to my ribs, I see all the bruising around my torso. I raise my eyebrows in surprise, I must have been so caught up in everything, that I forgot how sore I was. "It's okay, Zane. I'm safe now," I say, trying to reassure him.

He stands from the side of the bath, and smashes the wall with his fist. I flinch because I have had enough violence to last me a lifetime.

Walking up behind him, as he is leaning his hands on the wall, I wrap my arms around his torso. "It's okay, baby. Let's have a bath," I say to him, as I begin to pull off his cut; folding it, and placing it on the towel holder.

I proceed to remove his shirt, and once it has gone, I take a second to look at this magnificent body. It is as though every muscle that the human body is rippling out of him; as if he trains every single muscle. "Just get in the bath, Alaina," he replies, with pain in his voice.

As much as I like disobeying him, now is not the time. So I walk to the sink, get some candles out of the cupboard above the mirror, and begin placing them around the bath, lighting them one at a time before getting in. I instantly relax.

I glance over to Zane, who is now sitting on top of the closed toilet, shirtless, with just his jeans on. One of his hands are clasped around his mouth, as he stares at me with such intensity that it makes me uncomfortable. He has so much emotion in his stare, it gives me butterflies. I keep my eyes on him, and we just stare at each other for what feels like years, before he exhales out a rush of air.

He pulls his jeans down, I see his cock is half erect as he gets into the bath opposite me, and runs his wet hand over his hair. When I've finished washing myself and pruney, he still hasn't taken his eyes off me. The silence is stifling and I'm now at the point where I don't know what to do with myself, so I grab the towel deciding to leave him in his thoughts. They're obviously dark, very dark, and I'm unsure I don't want to interrupt them.

CHAPTER 18

ZANE

I'm sitting opposite the girl of my fucking dreams, the girl I know I'll be spending the rest of my life with, and all I am thinking about, is putting Shane Amaro back together, just so I can rip him apart all over again.

The bruise that covers her entire left torso area makes me want more blood. It's bad enough seeing her eyes dark and bruised. So at the moment, I can't talk, all I can do, is stare at the raw beauty sitting in front of me. Fuck she's amazing, her long blonde hair pulled back, those rosy cheeks from the steam of the bath, and her perfect green eyes, staring at me like they can see right through to my dark soul. I know this woman will be my undoing.

I stay in the same position, with my eyes locked on hers, until she rises. Water runs down her body as she reaches for a towel. Before she can hide her body from me, I lean out and grab her hand, slowly and gently pulling her back into me with water splashing everywhere. "Ugh, Zane!" she laughs.

I pull her into me, so her back is to my front, and I just inhale her scent, kissing her on the head. "I swear to you, baby, no one will ever come close enough to hurt you again, I'm sorry I didn't get there sooner."

She spins around and puts her hands on my chest. "Zane, it's not your fault okay? This is my shit."

I pull her hands off me, and kiss them. "Your shit is now my shit too, you're mine Alaina, and I will destroy anyone who hurts you."

She kisses me hard, pushing her perfect perky tits up against my chest, making my dick stand to life, even more than he was before.

Picking her up, and place her on top so she is straddling me. She moans, and tilts her head back. It is a fucking beautiful sound. There I go again, with that word—beautiful and I do not give a fuck, I would give my left nut just to be with this girl forever.

Kissing down her neck, making a trail down to her nipple's and placing each of them in my mouth, one at a time, with gentle suction, before picking her up out of the bath, with her legs still wrapped around me.

I place her on the bathroom sink, spreading her legs wide open for me. I step back, and take a look at her. "Fuck," I mumble, smirking at her.

Lowering to my knees, my head between her thighs, as my tongue takes over, licking her clit slowly, each stroke radiates through her body. As she arches her back in pleasure, I push one finger inside her hot wet opening, at the same time as I'm rubbing her nub in perfect slow circular motions. She's panting and gripping my head, so I pick up my pace, going faster and a little harder, before I feel her orgasm explode all over my finger.

I stand and smile at her, while I begin licking every little bit of her off me. Picking her up, placing her on her legs, I spin her around so she can see herself in the mirror.

"I'm not done with you yet, baby." Bending her over, I slam into her and she whips her head back, screaming out in pure pleasure. I twirl her long as fuck hair around my fist, pulling her head back; while I pound into her at a steady pace. "Look at me baby, look at me in the mirror," I say.

Her eyes find mine while I fuck her into oblivion, they start rolling back, so I nudge her hair a little. "Look at me when you come." I bring my hand to the front of her and start massaging her clit with added pressure. It's not long before I feel her body tense up, moaning in pleasure as she finishes up her second orgasm, and a couple thrusts later, I join her.

I pull out of her, slapping her ass. "Get back in the bath, babe." We both jump back into the bath, squirting shampoo into my palm, I begin to massage it into her scalp. She moans in approval, getting the attention of my dick immediately.

She laughs. "More?" asking me over her shoulder.

"Much more."

CHAPTER 19

ALAINA

It's nine am when I start to make my way down the hallway after waking with no Zane in the bed.

The smell of bacon and eggs hits my senses instantly, making my tummy rumble in approval. When I see Zane, he's flipping pancakes in nothing but baggy grey track pants. His glorious chest is out on display. All I want to do is watch him; he sure is a sight to see. His muscles ripple with each movement he makes.

I hear my mom and dad walk up behind me. "Alaina? Why are you standing in the doorway?" my father asks, as he is walking in. I hear my mom giggle, winking at me.

I almost forgot that I have a lot of lost time to make up for with these two. Zane turns around and smiles his full double dimple smile at me.

"Pervy are we?" he asked and I tilt my head.

"When it's you, always." He comes up and kisses me. "As long as it's only me." He walks back to the stove and focuses on the food. I roll my eyes at his possessiveness.

Blake and Ade walk through the door. "Oh brother, you shouldn't have," Ade says as he rubs his tummy, getting a piece of bacon.

We all sit out on the patio, eating our monster breakfast, enjoying the lush scenery of New Zealand. Behind our house, it's surrounded in bright green hills, it is so naturally beautiful. "So, when are we heading back?" I asked, in between bites. Unladylike, I know but this shit's amazing, and there is no way I'm stopping just to talk.

"The jet is on standby for whenever you are ready to head back," my father replies.

I look over to him. "Why do I get the feeling you're not coming?" He puts his knife and fork down, sparing a glance at my mother, before coming back to me. "Can we talk to you a minute, baby girl?" I nod and wipe my mouth, as we make our way to the swing set that hangs under my old tree house. I had it all as a child; but when I had to relocate to Westbeach, money was tight with my nana and pops. My dad is from

New Zealand but my mom is from America, so I stayed with her parents. I learnt that if you want nice things, you have to work for them; and I would not change that experience for any amount of money.

I sit on the swing, while both my parents stand in front of me. I still cannot believe that they are both alive, and I cannot begin to imagine the horrible stuff my mother would have gone through. My heart breaks for her. Even though I barely know them now, they are my parents, and all the memories I have of them are special.

"Well, you can talk when you're ready," I say smiling up at them.

CHAPTER 20

ALAINA

My father puts his hands in his pockets. "We're going to stay here Alaina, I can do my work from here, and New Zealand has always been our home."

I nod my head in approval and look over at my mom, who looks worried. "It's okay, I understand. I might spend the rest of the week here before heading back though."

They both smile at me. "We would really love that, darling."

"Mom?" I say, she is staring out into space.

"Yes? Sorry, baby, I'm listening."

I look to my dad and see his worried expression. He whispers something in her ear and she smiles at me before saying, "I better go clean up."

I look to my dad and he is still dazzling even in his old age. "I'm worried about your mother; I'm going to set her up with the best people in this country, to help her get through this."

"I know, daddy. It will take time. I can't imagine the horrendous things she would have had to live through."

He walks closer to me, and kisses my head. "I love you, princess, and don't ever forget that." Before he walks off to help my mom clean up.

"I never have, dad," I mumble to myself.

I sit there for a while, thinking of all the events that have unfolded throughout the past month, but in the end, these people right here, mean the world to me.

Dusting off my pants, I make my way back inside to take Jesse his breakfast; when Blake stops me in my tracks. "Hey, firecracker. I can't get hold of Vicky." Oh right, I forgot all about her plan to go to the ranch with her phone turned off.

I scribble down the number and pass it to him. "Call her, but please don't let her worry." He nods his head. I can see the secret happiness spread all over his face. Why the fuck can't they sort it out.

Getting a plate down from the cupboard, I start piling it up with food. "Is that for Jesse?"

Zane asks, walking up behind me and wrapping his arms around my waist.

"Yep, he must be starving," I respond, and I see him move around to stand and face me.

"As long as I don't need to remind him who you belong to, then we should be good."

I scoff. "I can assure you, nothing has ever happened between Jesse and me, but I do love him like a brother." He still does not look good with this; so I put down what I'm doing.

"Zane, I'm going to have other men in my life. A lot of them, are your men," I say, pointing outside to Ade in particular.

His eyes narrow as they fall on Ade. "Don't test me Alaina." I sigh, before continuing, "But —" walking directly in front of him, and wrapping my arms around his torso. "You're my everything. I worship your existence Zane."

He wraps his arms around me. "You'll be my old lady?" he asked, looking at me with complete seriousness.

"Yes, I accept," I say, and he looks back at me in shock.

"Are you serious?" he double checks, with a smile on his face.

"Zane, I thought you might have gotten it when I told you that I love you." He picks me up and lays the sweetest kiss on my lips. "Fuck I love you."

I smile at him. "I love you too, Zane." And he kisses me again.

He puts me back down and slaps my ass. "Go feed the boy."

And, he's back.

After giving Jesse his breakfast, I decide it is about time to change out of my pajamas, and watch a movie. I am looking through all our old DVDs in the theatre when Zane comes in.

"Movie day?" he asks, I bob my head up and down like a little kid. "I'll go get the popcorn, you find the movie," he says as he walks back out the room.

I love this Zane. This Zane is reserved for me only, and it makes me feel special. But I also know I have my work cut out for me. I keep looking through movies, when I see the one I want to watch. "Yes, Big Momma's House," I mumble under my breath. I still love this movie, it will always make me laugh.

Zane comes in and relaxes on the couch, looking up at me with his almost smile. I think aside from us having sex, his smile is my next favourite thing. He pats the spot next to him, so I sit down, stealing some popcorn and relaxing right by his side.

I must had fallen asleep, because I wake up alone on the couch, wondering when I dozed off. I stand to go and see where Zane is. When I walk into the conservatory, I see everyone in there.

"Hey, what's going on?" I ask, noticing all the worried faces.

"It's Jesse, darling, he needs to get to a hospital, but we can't have him in one here because too many people will ask questions, we need to send him back to LA, where I have people waiting for him," my father replies, waiting for my reaction.

"Okay," I say. "But I'm going with him."

Zane steps in. "No, you need to stay here and spend some time with your parents, he'll be fine."

Looking over to my moody man, I reply. "I'm going Zane, me and my parents have all the time in the world to see each other now." I smile at them as they return it.

My dad looks at me. "If it's what you want to do then that's fine, I can get you all on the same flight out tonight."

Then reality hits me, I'm leaving my parents again. "Give me a minute," I say, raising my finger, as I sit down and think over my options. "When will I see you next? Are you sure you're safe now?" I ask, as my dad sits next to me on the sofa.

"We will fly over next month, I promise, and I'll always visit you when I'm in the country." I nod, feeling a little better.

Zane stands up and *finally* agrees with me. "Okay, then we're going. I'll go pack up our stuff."

Once everyone has left the room, it is just my mom and me. She slowly sits next to me.

"I'm so sorry Alaina, I wish I could have done more, I just —" I raise my hand. "Stop mom, it's not your fault, please don't think any of this is your fault."

She looks at me and smiles. "Oh sweet girl, if you knew the story of how this started."

I stop her, because I realise I hadn't told mom or dad about the big pour out Shane had with me when I first got here. "Stop," I say softly. "I know, I know everything mom. Shane told me all of it. It's still not your fault. I would never walk away from Zane, so I get it; just please don't blame yourself, and maybe one day when you're ready, you can tell me what happened to you. I love you mom, so much. Just get better for me, and for dad, because my god, he loves you."

She looks at me with tears pouring down her cheeks, before pulling me into the tightest hug I have ever had, and that's saying something, having been in between Zane's monster arms. "Oh my sweet girl, thank you," she replies, and it looks as though a huge cloud has shifted off her. "I didn't know how I was going to start explaining it to you."

I smile. "It's okay mom, it's time to heal now." I squeeze her back just as my dad walks in, he looks at both of us and smiles a knowing smile. "The jet's ready, I can drive you all."

Getting to my feet, I give her another hug. "I love you mom, I'll see you real soon okay?"

"I love you too, sweetheart."

"Alright, I think we're ready."

I start to walk towards the stairs, when I see Zane walking in with our bags. "How's Jesse coming?" I asked, looking between Zane and my dad.

My dad turns to me. "My assistant will drive him in another car, so he can lie down."

"Okay," I reply, as we make our way to the truck.

I see Ollie and Felix bring Jesse out, laying him in the car in front of us. I get into the passenger seat, with my dad in the drivers, while Zane, Blake, Ade, Ollie, and Felix are riding their bikes. We begin to pull out, following closely behind Jesse, with the boys riding behind us. I take in the beauty of New Zealand for one last time. The fresh air, the green trees, and beautiful nature. It's not long before we are on the airstrip and this will all be a memory.

Getting out of the truck, it is freezing, so Zane automatically takes his hoodie off, pulling it on me. I look ridiculous, like I'm wearing a thick, big, black dress with Sinful Souls MC on the front, but I don't care, I just want Jesse better.

Turning to face my dad, I notice the worry lines etched all over his face. "I'll always have eyes on you, you know that right?" he says and I giggle, because he is cute when he worries. "I'm serious Alaina, and for the record, I trust Zane. He's a hard man yes, but he loves you, I see it and I respect it. It is why I am not begging you to stay."

I stand on my tippy toes, and lay a kiss on his cheek. "I love you dad, try not to worry too hard, you're starting to get wrinkles."

His face changes, and he smiles before yelling, "Love you too, baby girl."

I look over to Blake as he comes up next to me, making our way on to the waiting jet. "Ready to face Vicky's wrath?" he asks me. *Oh boy, I forgot about this.*

"As I'll ever be," I respond. The girl scares the shit out of me.

CHAPTER 21

ZANE

My nerves are getting the best of me, I can't believe I'm going to ask a girl to marry me. I've obviously lost my fucking mind ...

7 hours earlier

"Big Momma's house? Really?" I said to her. Nothing about this girl surprised me anymore, *except maybe when she gunned down three men with perfect aim—that scared the fucking shit out of me.*

We were sitting on the sofa about to begin the movie, but it was not long after the opening credits that she fell fast asleep on my lap. I've had this thought since I knew I was going to make her my old lady. I knew I was going to marry her, but I wanted to make it as special as I could.

I got a text from Harvey yesterday, but only read it this morning:

> Harvey: *Hey brother, hope everything is going smooth over there and you are not having too much fun without the rest of us. Thought I'd let you know, Bianca signed the papers today and dropped them off along with an early paternity test that she had done stating, you are NOT the father, count your lucky stars my brother, you dodged a fucking bullet.*

With my focus here, I'd forgotten all about the drama back home. The minute Alaina was taken, she became my only focus, but it made me realise I want those things eventually, and I'll only ever want them with Alaina.

Slowly picking her head up off my lap, and placing it on the couch. I grabbed a blanket and pulled it over her; kissing her head softly before I went to find Joseph. I found him talking to a doctor down the hallway; he excused himself from her before coming to me.

"Everything okay?" I asked, pointing to the doc.

"Not really, Jesse isn't looking too good. He may need to go home earlier than we thought. We are prepping things now."

I thought about that for a second, and I know Alaina is going to want to pack up and go with him. So that crossed out plan A. "Can I talk to you a sec? In private?" I asked, and he nodded his head as I began to follow him to his office.

I was sitting back on the seat in his office, jiggling my legs out of nervousness, before just blowing it out and saying it. "I want to marry Alaina, I guess I should ask for your blessing out of respect for you. I would want the same from my daughter."

Just when I thought he was going to say something, he smiled a huge smile at me. A genuinely happy smile. Not a 'I'm about to murder you' smile. He rose and came over to pat me on my back. "I couldn't think of a better man for her Zane, just look after her."

I laughed, I could think of one hundred men that would be better for her; too bad they will never have a chance, because after I wife her, I'm gonna Mom her. "I appreciate that Joseph, I'm going to head into town while she's asleep, find a ring. Do you want to come?"

"It's a good thing you asked that while here in New Zealand, I know just the ring."

Pulling up to Mitchel & Co, I felt nervous. Was I actually fucking doing this? But then I thought of her and all doubt washed out of my mind. I wanted her, for the rest of my life.

I felt a kick come from the back seat. The person occupying the seat behind me happened to be the annoying Ade. He refused to stay home once he found out what we were going to do. "What do you want, Ade?" I asked in a flat tone.

"I love you, and respect you, because you're my brother and my president. But if you hurt her, I won't think twice about chopping your dick off; Just sayin'," he said, throwing his hands up. I had to give it to him, I know he means well for Alaina, and as much as it annoys the living shit out of me—*and fuck does it annoy me*—they both have this fucked up bond. I can live with it, because I know with all the stupid fucking flirting aside, Ade would not even breathe in Alaina's direction, because he knows I'll gut him like a fish in his sleep. "Fuck up Ade and get your ass out of the car."

Walking in, I saw Joseph talking to an older woman; she looked to be in her late sixties. I began making my way to her. "Lily, this is Zane, he's my future son in law. That is granting, my daughter accepts his proposal." Joseph said with a smirk. "Word." Ade laughed in the background, before shutting up when he sees the look I'm giving him.

I placed my hand out, "Nice to meet you, Lily," she smiled at me, shaking my hand before turning her attention back to Joseph.

"I have the piece, I completed it once she left, hoping one day she would come back to her roots." I looked questioning at Joseph as Lily walked out.

Five minutes later, she came back in, holding a gold envelope. I took it, and opened it carefully before pulling out what had to be the best-looking ring I'd ever seen. It's perfect for my girl. "It's perfect."

It's gold, with a diamond the size of my pinkie nail sitting on it, and around the diamond are two perfect little hearts. They look to be made out of some sort of stone.

"The diamond is a half carat princess cut diamond—because she's always been my little princess," Joseph said, smiling at it before he continued. "The stones in the shape of the hearts are Kawakawa Pounamu, or in other words; green stone. The green stone has been collected from her lake in the South Island of New Zealand, where my family is from." He carried on. "The gold has been melted down out of my mother and father's gold wedding bands, to create one; they loved each other until their very last breath. When my mother passed away, my father passed away from a heart attack right after finding out, I always knew that when, and if, Alaina ever found an everlasting love; I wanted her to have them...so I had them melted together."

I had no words. This ring was perfect. It held so much irreplaceable value, as Alaina was to me. "Thank you Joseph, I mean it. This...means a fucking lot."

He put his hands in his pockets. "I know everlasting love when I see it." I nodded and looked back to Lily. "I'll take it."

After trying to give money to either Joseph or Lily, I ended up dropping five thousand cash on the counter before walking out. I knew that in no way did that even come close to how much this was worth, but it was the last of what I had left in cash on me.

That brings us to now, where I'm sitting next to her on our way back to Westbeach to face the rest of the world. I kiss her head, and close my eyes, feeling a little circle burning through my pockets.

CHAPTER 22

ALAINA

After a long flight, I have jet lag and I need my bed. Seeing a limo waiting for us, I follow Zane as he makes his way over to it. The driver comes out and he is a tall, thick, African American man with a friendly face.

"Smith," Zane nods to him when we get there. "Can you take Alaina straight to her place?"

I look to Zane before asking, "You're not coming with me?" He looks distant, and he is acting strange.

"No, I've got shit to sort Alaina, just do as you're told. I'll text you later, get some rest baby," he softens his tone towards the end of his sentence. *Isn't that a sign of schizophrenia?*

"O-okay then," I take my bag off him and jump into the back.

Pulling away from Zane and the boys, I feel empty, *talk about being attached.* The drive there gives me time to think about what I had done, something's obviously crawled up his ass.

I look over to Smith, "Do you work for my dad?"

He looks into his vision mirror. "Yes, ma'am."

I scoff, "Please hold up on the ma'am, it makes me feel old."

He smiles. "Yes, Alaina."

His friendly tone makes me relax. "Thank you."

When we pull up to campus, I'm reminded of all my responsibilities. I need to finish up my exams so I can graduate. Lucky I'm in my final year.

"Thanks, Smith."

"No problem," he responds, getting out with my bag, and closing the door behind me.

I start to make my way to my room, feeling homesick. I feel like this isn't my home anymore, my home is where Zane is.

Opening my door, I'm greeted by a very worried Vicky. "LAIN!!! OH MY GOD!" she yells, running up, squeezing me.

I notice her tummy has grown, so I rub my hand over it. "Vicky! This is your decision?" she looks at me then places her hand over mine. "It is Lain, I want this baby, our baby. Only thing is, I don't know how I'm going to break it to him."

I put my bags down. "Well, you better do it soon, because we're all back and he's on a mission to track you down."

Her eyes drop to the floor and she wrings her hands. "I know."

She looks up, and I see her happy face has been replaced with an angry one. *Oh boy, here we go.* "I can't fucking believe it, Alaina, you could have died! Tell me everything, right now."

I nod my head in agreement, before saying, "First, I need wine, and pizza."

She turns around, following my movements. "Pizza? You hate pizza."

I look to her. "When you've had to go through not being fed, you would love all kinds of food too," she pulls two glasses out of the cupboard as I'm ordering the pizza.

Thirty minutes later, we are sitting in front of the TV, eating pizza and drinking wine out of our cheap wine glasses. It feels like old times. Well, me drinking wine, her drinking water. I bring the glass to my lips but the smell is off and I put it back on the table.

"So, talk!" she demands.

I put my food down and spill everything out to her, from start to finish.

"Oh my god, is Jesse going to be okay? I can't believe it, it's like I have a sign on my head saying use me to get to Alaina Vance." She says rolling her eyes.

I laugh. "Don't be silly, he was working for my dad all along."

"I can't believe your father is some huge leader of the killer world, you're pretty badass! And your mom is alive, that's so beautiful Lain, I'm so happy for you."

She has no idea how badass I am, but I might just leave the little shooting incident back in New Zealand. "I'm really happy right now, do you want ice cream?" I ask her, and she stops pizza mid-air. "Ice cream?"

I look to her. "Yeah, want some? I've still got some caramel in here somewhere," I say while rummaging through the freezer. There is silence. "Vick?" I ask, turning to find her staring at me. "Don't look at me like that, it's making me feel fat."

She laughs before saying, "When was your last period?" What the hell kind of question is that.

"What? I don't know, the night before I met Zane was when I finished," whispering the last bit of my sentence. "Fuck." There is no way, I mean, I got beaten quite severely, so if I was I would have miscarried, *surely*. "No way, keep your pregnancy bugs to yourself. I'm nowhere near ready for that shit."

"Because of study? You finish up in two months, Alaina. You have a man that is head over heels in love with you and you can always come back to it. You could be worse off, for instance, having to drop school and hide the pregnancy from the dad because you know he never actually wanted you."

I look to her and my heart breaks for her situation. "Vicky, you need to speak to Blake, the way I see it, he does want you. Just talk to him please, and get a jacket."

She stands; shoving the last bit of pizza in her mouth like it is her last meal. "Why?" She asks.

Grabbing the keys off the kitchen counter. "I'm going to need a pregnancy test."

CHAPTER 23

ZANE

Being at the clubhouse has me back in my element. I fucking miss my girl like crazy though, I need her with me twenty-four seven. Picking up my phone, I dial her number and she picks up on the third ring.

"Hey baby," she purrs down the phone; resulting in my dick twitching in response. *He knows his owners voice.*

"Hey darling, you busy?" I ask, and silence fills the line.

"Uh, um, no, not really." Her tone sounding off.

I get to my feet, and as if she can sense my worry. "Calm down Zane, I'm safe and fine." "I miss you, want to come up here?" I ask her.

"I might just stay here tonight, it's been a long day, and I need to sort out my final exams tomorrow so I can just be done with college." What the fuck?

"What about tomorrow?"

She stutters. "Uh." Yeah, I have had enough of this conversation.

"Alaina, that wasn't a question. Sort through your shit tomorrow, I'll be there at midday."

She sighs. "Okay baby, I love you." My body relaxes every time she says those three words. She is the calm in my storm.

"I love you too."

Hanging up my phone, I'm thinking what the fuck that was about, something was off. There's no way I'm waiting until tomorrow to see her.

After sorting through some club shit, I find myself at Alaina's dorm. Walking up to her door and about to knock, when it's opened by Vicky.

"Oh, Zane. Sorry, I thought you were Blake."

Looking down at the bump in front of her, I point. "Blake's?" she scrunches her eyes closed before nodding.

"Good luck with that," I respond, as I stalk towards Alaina's bedroom. I'm not sure how Blake is going to respond to that, but I wish her fucking luck.

Opening it, I find her with her knees pulled up, and her head resting on her knees. She must hear the door open because her eyes shoot up, all red from crying.

"Fuck," I mumble, closing the door behind me and sliding in next to her.

I pull her into me. "Baby, what's wrong?" Silence, filled with more silence, until eventually she opens her mouth but only a whisper comes out.

"I'm pregnant, Zane." A wave of relief washes over me, calming my speedy mind. Then reality sets in fuck, I am going to be a dad and I cannot be happier.

"Are you serious?" I ask her, with a huge smile spread across my face.

She looks at me and laughs. "Why are you happy?"

I wipe the tears away from her eyes. "Babe, there is nothing that would make me happier, than having a child with you. Well, maybe one other thing. I was going to wait until I had thought up some corny shit, but ..." I get down on my knee, with her hand in my palm.

"Marry me, baby?" I ask, fishing the ring out of my pocket.

She nods her head up and down, while her arms fly around my neck. "Yes!" She's crying again, but I think these are happy tears.

Sliding the ring down her finger. "Oh my god, it's beautiful, Zane!" I smile and explain the whole story to her that her dad told me. Her eyes look up into mine, showing nothing but raw love. "I love you so much sexy biker number two," she says, cheekily.

My face drops, "Number two? What the fuck?"

She giggles her cute as fuck giggle. "Long story."

CHAPTER 24

ALAINA

I wake to the early morning sun blazing through my window, with Zane fast asleep next to me; his face relaxed. God, he really is perfect, and he's all mine. The thought makes my insides melt.

I look at the ring on my finger, and it makes me want to cry all over again. It's so beautiful, and special. I'm the luckiest girl in the world; with Zane and peanut, we are going to be our own little family, *oh how my life has changed.*

Pulling the covers off my side, trying not to wake him, and get up to start on breakfast before classes. I have so much to sort out.

Making my way into the kitchen, I turn our sound dock on, plugging in my iPod while a

Kanye West song comes blasting through the sound system.

I get whisking some eggs and frying some bacon, I want waffles and maple syrup too. This pregnancy thing has me in love with food, all I want to do is eat. I make a decision right then, that I need to make time for a jog/walk today, while secretly hoping my mother's tiny genes will count while I am pregnant.

"Ugh, that noise!" Blake comes in, pulling his hair dramatically, with his jeans on, *and only his jeans on.* I take a second to check him out, because, hey, I am still a normal girl, with normal eyes; and he is packing nicely.

He must notice my gawking because his body stills. "Lain, you trying to get us both killed? Stop staring at me like that, and put some proper fucking music on, will you. This shit is killing me." I giggle because he is right, Zane would lose his shit.

"Waffles?" I ask, and he smiles. "Yes, fuck yes."

I look over to him. "So I take it Vicky broke the news to you then?"

He laughs while pouring a coffee. "What? That she's eaten one too many burgers while I've been gone?" My eyes widen, shit, has she really not told him. "Relax Alaina, I'm joking, I know she's pregnant. We just have to figure out how we are going to do this while not being together," he says, clearly annoyed.

I look to him, "Why? Why can't you be together?"

He sits down coffee in hand. "Because she deserves better, and she's not for me."

I drop my eyes. "Blake, you're an idiot."

He laughs, "Yeah, maybe, but it still has to be done."

Just then, Vicky comes walking in, "The music Lain, turn it off, my ears are bleeding." I forget how much of a rock goddess and purest my friend is.

I laugh. "Chill guys, it's just music, and if I'm cooking, then I pick. Now shut up and sit."

I begin dishing out breakfast when Zane walks in, fresh out the shower with no top on. He's wearing ripped baggy jeans while still drying his hair.

He wraps the towel around his neck, and I blush, wanting to jump his sexy bones. I peer over to Vicky, noticing her eyes glued on him. "Wow Mathews, you really know how to get a girl going in the morning." She makes no motions to hide the fact that she's licking her lips.

I narrow my eyes and smirk, looking over to Blake, to see his face blank, with his mouth set in a hard line. *She's not for you, my left ass cheek.*

"Morning baby," he says, kissing me on the lips.

"Morning, I made a bit of everything because I've decided I'm okay with being a fat bitch for life. Now, tell me you love me."

He smiles while saying on my lips, kissing me after every word. "I. Love. You."

I smile while he takes a seat by Blake. "Good, there's no way out now."

"Don't care, I love me some curves." I roll my eyes because all guys say that.

After finishing breakfast, the boys start on the dishes while Vicky and I go to get ready. "Lain?" Vicky says from behind me.

"Yeah? You okay?" I ask.

She looks to the side, "Yeah, yeah I'll be fine— Oh my god! Is that a ring?" she screams.

I see the boys stop what they are doing, while Blake squeezes Zane on the shoulder, congratulating him. When I look back to Vicky, she's crying.

"Vicky, it's okay."

She looks at me. "No, I know I'm being silly, and I'm so happy for you. When's the big day?"

We start talking about dates and dresses, when I glance a look at Zane and Blake, their eyes are huge, as they mumble something that sounds a lot like "fucking women" before getting back to their appointed chores.

"I'm thinking I want it after the baby, when I can fit back into a size eight."

She bobs her head up and down. "I would really appreciate that also." Rubbing her growing belly.

I put my hand over hers. "How far along are you now?"

She wipes the tears under her eyes. "Seven months." She has no idea how amazing she looks for seven months pregnant; I can only hope I look as good as she does.

"Not long now," I hug her, before we go to our rooms to get ready for the day.

CHAPTER 25

ALAINA

It's just after lunch when I finish sorting through all my papers. So I decide I want to go and see Jesse at the hospital. It has been a few weeks now since everything went down, but Jesse has had to have a few surgeries done since being back. One being when they had to operate on his around his brain because the protective tissue was severely damaged. Gathering up all my books and putting them in my bag, I swing it over my shoulder. Taking a bite out of my apple, I make my way to the student car park where my little Mazda 3 hatchback is parked. I love my car, even though I don't get to drive her often.

I get into the driver's seat and turn the key, before making my way to the hospital.

Pulling up, I park my car and head into the main reception area. "I'm here to see Jesse Armenta," I say to the nurse, as looks through her computer. "Room sixteen, sweetheart." I begin walking toward his room. I have never liked hospitals, they freak me out.

Finding Jesse's room, I see him sitting up, and eating a bag of Doritos while watching TV. He has a five o'clock shadow, and his hair has grown out a bit.

"Hey J," I say, and when he spots me he smiles.

"Hey Lain, you didn't have to come see me."

I jump into the bed next to him, stealing his bag of chips. "Don't be stupid, of course I did. How are you feeling?"

He turns the TV off. "Way better, just got banged up a bit, few broken ribs, no biggie. I'll be back on the court before you know it," he says with a wink.

I laugh, "You just work on getting better, Kobe Bryant." As I snuggle into him, telling him everything that has happened since we got back.

"You're pregnant! And getting married?" he asks in complete shock.

I nod my head. "Yep, big changes huh!"

He laughs. "Yeah huge! Congrats Lain."

We continue eating, and I stay for a couple hours, just talking with him. Before deciding to head back home.

Once I walk in the door, Zane's there on the couch.

"Hey guys," I say, walking in and dropping my bag on the floor.

Zane makes his way over to me. "Hey baby, where have you been?" he asks, kissing me.

"I went to see Jesse for a couple hours, fill him in and all that," he stills, before relaxing again. He will get use to sharing my friendship one of these days, all in good time.

"Where's Vick?" I ask, looking over to Blake.

"She's gone for a scan, wouldn't let me go. She says I can't pick and choose when I want to be involved, but the thing is, I want to be involved with my kid, just not so much with her."

I start taking my jacket off. "You know, one of these days you need to stop lying to yourself, B." I can't stand to be in the same room with him without wanting to start foaming at the mouth and attack him. I shake my head before heading to my bedroom.

Zane's hot on my heels and closes the door behind him. "Move in with me."

I look over to him, "Pardon?" because I do not think I quite caught that.

"Not to the clubhouse, to my house down town. Let's do it now." I want this, so bad, but now I am worried about Vicky. I sit on the edge of the bed and shuck my shoes off.

"What about Vicky? I can't leave her. She's going through all sorts of shit right now," I say, as he closes the door.

"Me and Blake have already spoken, she'll be moving in with him until she's had the baby." Somehow, I just don't see that happening, so I laugh.

"Yeah, I want front seats to that show."

Zane sits down on the bed next to me. "I'm serious Alaina, move in with me."

I look at him for a brief moment and then nod. I don't need time to think about this. It feels right. "Okay." He pulls me in for a kiss, before starting to pack everything. "Oh you mean like right now, move in with you?"

Zane smiles over his shoulder but doesn't stop pulling out a suitcase and duffle bag. "Why wait?"

I shake my head and pull out my phone, I decide to ring Vicky.

"Hey Vick, can you talk?" I ask. She must be driving because I hear the car pull over.

"Yep, now I can. What's up?" *Oh this is going to go great.*

"Lain, if this is about Zane asking you to move in with him, do it...I heard him and Blake talking, and I think it's a good idea. You need this." *Oh thank god.*

"But are you going to be okay?"

She laughs. "Of course! I'm fabulous darling, don't you worry." I burst out laughing, I really do love this crazy girl.

"Okay. I'll see you later, love you."

"Love you too, Lain."

I hang up the phone, and make my way back into my room. "Let's go then, I'll need to go through everything and pack it up."

He smiles and picks me up. "You don't need anything, I have everything." I'm reminded that I have not seen his house, but I'm going to marry him, and have a kid with him; I must be crazy.

"Sounds good, I'll just get all my bathroom necessities then," I reply, as we both start packing everything up. I stop before the bathroom and get all my photos that I have around my room. Snapshots into my wild nights. That chapter of my life is over, but a new one is about to begin, and I cannot be happier.

We pull up to a two storey white house, complete with a wraparound porch and guarded in by a tall fence. There's a tree in the front yard that would be perfect to hang a swing off too, it's tidy and nice. I had no idea Zane had this sort of money.

"Wow," I say, jumping out of his black Escalade. "Zane, it's beautiful."

He smiles. "You like it?"

"I love it, I seriously had no idea you had this sort of money."

He looks to me. "It's not dirty if that's what you're asking, I own a couple of completely legitimate businesses in town. One of them being ZM Automotive. And I've just purchased a building in town, planning to turn it into a nightclub."

I look at him with my eyebrows raised. "I'm impressed."

He laughs. "Well, at least I know you're not with me for my money." He gently swats my hand away as he starts pulling all my bags out of the back.

"Nope, just your sexy dick." He stills, with complete shock in his expression.

"Holy fuck women, you floor me." I laugh while following him.

Walking to the front door. "Are you sure a woman doesn't live here?" I ask. The man is seriously tidy for a biker.

"The only woman that comes here every now and then, is my mother." I smile at the mention of his mother, she's is such a beautiful, angelic woman.

Walking in, directly in front of me is the stair case leading to upstairs, and to the left of that, is a hallway leading to a room at the back end of the house. To the right, there is a complete glass-sliding door where there looks to be a huge—and I mean huge, gym set up. *Holy fuck.*

We walk to the left, into a massive lounge area. It's complete with an oversized L shaped black leather sofa, and the biggest state of the art television I have ever seen hanging on the wall. The walls are painted black and red. *Yep definitely a man's home here.*

I walk into the kitchen, where it is all black marble benchtops with stainless steel appliances.

"Wow," I say, as he is watching me intently. "You decorate all this?" He nods. "It's amazing."

I carry on through the kitchen, down to the room at the back end of the house. You can access it through the kitchen, or through the hallway. Turning the light on, I see it is a dining room, and like every other room, it is long and very large. With a long, wooden table that could seat at least twelve people comfortably; and on the far right wall, sits a large gas fireplace. The entire back wall is one big ceiling to floor glass sliding door, which opens out to the back yard.

He walks over to the door, unlocking it, and sliding it right across, giving it the perfect indoor, and outdoor entertainment flow. Stepping onto the enormous porch, I take in everything.

"Oh my god, Zane," I say. There's a huge pool in the middle, that has lights lighting the water up, and a spa pool connected onto it. I make my way out, and find there is a completely different area out here, with a huge BBQ and bar area that has backyard lights draping around everything, lighting up the whole place.

There is a large stone, outdoor setting under a sail, and the gardens are so well maintained.

I look over to him. "It's so beautiful just, wow." It really is truly amazing.

"Come, I'll show you the bedrooms," he replies, as I follow him back into the house.

We make our way up the stairs, and directly in front of the stairs is a door. Opening it, he says, "This is the master bedroom. Our bedroom. I wanted it directly there so I can keep an eye on everything." This doesn't surprise me at all.

When he opens the door, I'm greeted by a huge bedroom. All dark greys and whites, with a huge king sized bed; another large TV hanging on the wall opposite the bed, and a few drawers scattered nicely around the room.

He opens the wardrobe. "You can have this, until I get another one put in." Then he walks over to the bathroom, with me following close behind. It is laid out beautifully with his and hers bench area, along with a big claw bathtub. Wow, I stare in complete awe.

"There's three other bedrooms down the hallway, I was thinking the one closest to us can be turned into the nursery."

I look up at him. "I'll go shopping for that tomorrow."

He starts pulling out his wallet. "Yep, with our accounts." He passes me a black card.

"Are you kidding, there's no way, Zane. You've done enough."

"It's me and you now baby, what's mine is yours."

I begin to fidget my fingers. "I...I don't know. It's all a little too much. I have a trust account I can use until I feel comfortable enough to spend your money."

He looks like he wants to argue, but he settles. "Okay, baby, whatever makes you happy."

Pulling me by my arm. "Now come here," he grabs me and picks me up, before laying me softly on the bed, and making sweet love to me all night long.

I am up early the next morning, trying to find everything in the kitchen. I begin pulling out things to make for breakfast when I see Zane walk in, all sweaty in sweatpants with no top.

"Hungry?" I ask, while I am mixing the waffle batter.

He pulls out a bar stool. "Starving."

"You go for a run?"

He shakes his head. "Gym. The whole right side of the house is laid out with everything you will ever need."

I smile up at him. "Just how rich are you, Mathews?"

He smirks. "Oh, you have no idea. Not yet anyway," he says getting up to get a vitamin water out of the fridge.

We finish up our breakfast, and I think I ate enough for the both of us. I look up at Zane while I put a piece of fruit in my mouth. "What?" smiling around my maple syrup drizzled strawberry.

He smiles at me. "We're definitely having a boy."

I laugh and pop the strawberry in my mouth. "Shut up, and what if it's a girl?"

He stills, before shaking his head. "Nope, no way. I want a boy first, to be my eyes and ears when I'm not around."

I laugh. "More kids?"

He grins. "At least three."

I stop eating, shocked by his answer. "Yeah, not going to happen, biker."

He laughs and grabs my hand. "Come, I'll show you the rest of the house."

After showing me the gym that is completely full of all the latest equipment, a huge TV, and a monster sound system, he's seriously loaded. He takes me out the back, and I can see everything clearly now. It is just as stunning out here during the day, as it is during the night. I think it's my most favourite part of the house.

I'm lounging on one of the sun beds, when I get a text.

> Vicky: *What you doing?*
> Me: *Lounging by the pool.*

Remembering I need to go nursery shopping, I text her again.

> Me: *Care to shop?*
> Vicky: *Like you have to ask, what's the address? I'll come get you.*

I text her Zane's—well I guess it is my address too, as I make my way inside.

Zane is coming down the stairs, decked out in his white T-shirt, nicely fit jeans, combat boots and his cut. I almost forgot who my man was.

"Gotta head into the clubhouse, I might not be home until later. I'm sorry, baby."

I wave my hand. "No it's okay, Vicky's on her way over, we're going shopping." I wiggle my eyebrows.

He laughs. "Okay baby, I'll see you around five." He kisses me on the lips and gently runs his hand over my stomach. "Love you both."

Fifteen minutes later, the door opens and Vicky walks in. "Holy fuck."

"I know," I say to her, as she starts walking around the entire house.

"No. Like, holy actual fuck, Lain. This is some serious money." I nod my head because I know. However, it is all very casual rich; not over the top, flashy rich, which is perfect.

"I'll show you the, to-be nursery, then we can head out." She claps her hands excited.

I stop, and look at her. "Don't get too excited, I don't want you to go into early labour."

She laughs, then her laugh dies out. She looks at me all serious. "You're completely right."

We open the door, looking into the empty room. It's a light grey colour, with the curtains pulled open. It gets so much sun.

"It's beautiful," Vicky says.

"Sure is, shall we go?" We walk out the door, laughing and talking as we used to, before heading into town to shop up a storm.

CHAPTER 26

ALAINA

After Vicky and I shopped until we physically could not anymore, we came home and laid out by the pool, leaving all my expenditures in the nursery.

"How are you feeling?" I ask her.

"Like a huge, fat, whale...with cankles, and do you know the last time I could even see my vagina Lain? I'm serious. Pregnancy blows, but I can't wait to meet her."

I'm still laughing from the vagina comment, when I stop chewing the grape in my mouth. "HER? We're having a girl!" I jump up in glee.

She smiles, and nods her head up and down. "Yep we sure are, found out at my scan yesterday."

I hug her tightly. "She's going to be beautiful like her Mama." Vicky is drop dead gorgeous.

"Not right now, I'm not." She laughs while getting to her feet. "I better go, Blake will be home soon, and no doubt freak out wondering where I am. Not because of me, but because of the baby; all I am is a walking incubator for his baby girl," she says sadly.

I reach out and give her a hug. I wish I could make it better but they are both as pig headed as each other. They really are very similar and if they could get past this, they would make an awesome team. I pat her back as her baby girl gives a mighty kick.

Stepping back, I look down at her stomach before we both burst out laughing. "That hurt me so that must have hurt you."

Vicky rubs her stomach. "She's going to be a ball buster."

"Just like her momma," I say and walk her to the door. I give her one more hug before she gets into her car.

I look at the time and decide I had better get dinner started anyway. "Okay, I'll see you later," I say as I wave her off.

Padding barefoot into the kitchen, I pull some stuff out of the fridge, settling on chicken parmesan, when a sharp pain shoots right through my stomach.

I cry out in pain, holding my stomach in my hands, while making my way to the bathroom. *What the fuck was that.* I go to take a pee and notice there is blood all over my underwear.

"Oh fuck. No. No. NO!"

I throw on something new, when another cramp comes piercing into my stomach. I begin to cry, because *I know*. I know that this cannot be good. The amount of blood, and the severity of these cramps is not a good sign.

I search for my phone through my bag, and dial Zane's number, he picks up on the second ring. "Hey baby I'm almost home —"

I stop him with a sob as I try to breathe through the pain. "Zane, UGH —" another pain courses through my stomach.

"ALAINA!" I hear him yell down the phone.

"Zane something's wrong, I'm bleeding and I'm getting cramps."

"Fuck! I'm on my way baby, call the ambulance." Hanging up the phone, I begin dialling 911.

When they come through the door, I'm curled up in the fetal position on the floor. I can feel wetness between my legs, and I'm shaking in shock. *I don't want to lose our baby.*

Before I know it, I am being wheeled out on a gurney, and just as they're about to shut the doors, I hear Zane's bike pulling up.

"WAIT!" I scream. Zane swings open the ambulance doors, just in time.

"It's okay, he's my fiancé," I say, as they make room for him next to me. I look deep into his eyes and see nothing but fear.

He rubs my forehead. "It's okay baby, I'm here."

I take hold of his hand and silently pray for everything to be alright.

As soon as we get to the hospital, they move me into a room while they run all the tests. Once Zane and I are alone, I whisper to him, "This isn't good Zane, not good at all."

He grasps my hand into his. "I know, I know. But we will get through it."

Just then, the doctor comes through the door frowning, and I immediately know what she's going to say. She opens her mouth to speak, but I beat her to it.

"Don't. Just...Don't." Tears start streaming out of my eyes.

"I'm so sorry, Miss Vance." There it is. Shane Amaro had to take one final thing away from me that I had.

A sob bursts out of me and Zane gets up from his seat, getting into bed with me with bloodshot eyes. "We'll get through this baby." I only just found out I was pregnant a few days ago yes, but I fell in love with it and if my calculations were correct, I would have only just passed the six week mark—the safe mark. All the dreams and hopes for this baby, will never happen. I curse myself for getting swept up in the fantasy of happy families for it to shatter my heart. I've lost my baby. My precious baby. I can't give Zane the thing he was so over the moon to have. I look up at his pain stricken face and it breaks my heart more. My weeping sends me into a deep, dark, sleep.

When I wake, the whole club is in my room.

I smile as I sit up in my bed. "Hey guys." These big, beautiful, monsters are a sight to see.

A whole lot of apologies go round the room, and even though I don't have my baby anymore, when it's time, my time will come again; I just have to take it day by day.

Ade comes over to me, taking hold of my hand and kissing it. "I'm sorry, firecracker."

I smile a weak smile at him. "I know."

The boys stay for a couple hours, until Vicky is kicking them all out. She's not fazed at all that they all tower over her.

I laugh. "I think they're a little scared of you." She comes back over to my bed, trying to shoo Zane out of the way, only for him to look up to her with an annoyed 'Like fuck' look on his face. She rolls her eyes, walking in front of him anyway.

Pulling me forward, she fluffs up my pillow. "They should be, now get some rest and I'll be back tomorrow." She leans over and kisses me on the forehead before leaving.

The rest of the day goes slow, with just me and Zane lying on the bed. The doctor said I could go home tomorrow morning, depending on how I am feeling, but the worst of it should be over, providing I do not get an infection.

Before I know it, it's night out and all I want to do is close my eyes. I fall asleep with the thought that, one day, I might be privileged enough to have Zane's baby.

The next morning I feel a lot better physically, enough to go home, so I pack up all my stuff with Zane's help. Everyone's been asking how I'm feeling but no one asks him. He's lost his baby too and every time I approach the subject, he shuts me down. He's clearly in pain and he won't let me help him. He's trying to be strong but I can see him breaking.

Walking back through the reception, I sign out before we make our way to the truck, heading home in silence.

He looks over to me every second. "Are you going to be okay?"

"That's funny. I was going to ask you the same question." He looks at me and gives a frustrated huff. It's not the answer he wants to hear. "As okay as you get I guess." Feeling like a piece of me is missing.

When we pull up to the house, Zane opens my door.

"Come on baby, let's get you inside." He attempts to pick me up.

"Zane, my feet are fine. Stop being silly." Side stepping around him.

As soon as I am inside, I go straight to the bedroom and sit on the bed.

"You know it's going to be okay, it fucking hurts, I know, but there will be other times. And it gives us some more time with just me and you."

I look up to him with tears in my eyes. I'm surprised to see the tears in his eyes too. "It's so fucking hard, Zane. I'm sorry I've done this to you."

He pulls me into him, while I cry all over his shoulder while he releases his pain.

The next morning, I wake to find the bed empty, so I make my way downstairs where Zane is busy on the phone, so I start to busy myself with making a coffee.

He hangs up the phone, and hugs me from behind. "I want to bounce something off you real quick," he says.

I turn in his embrace while drinking my coffee. "Yes?"

He puts his hands in *those* grey track pants that I love so much. "What if I say we should push up the date of the wedding?" I stop mid drink, and put my cup down.

"I would say that's crazy, but let's do it." It's just what I need. Something to busy myself, and I get to marry the man that I love more than anything.

His face lights up. "Really? You agree to this?"

I smile and kiss him. "Of course I do."

He fist pumps the air and I laugh. "What the hell was that?"

He laughs back at me. "That was me finally being able to *legally,* lay claim on my women!" *Oh—now this man cares about the law.*

EPILOGUE

Three months later...

"Seriously Lain, you couldn't push this day a month later? A month, that's all I would have needed." I roll my eyes at her because she is being dramatic.

"Vicky, you look fucking amazing, and you have a beautiful baby girl."

Her face lights up like Christmas when I mention Pipper. "I do, don't I?" I nod my head.

Pipper is the most beautiful little baby in the world, and I am not just saying that because she is my god-daughter either. I had a cry when I first held her in my arms. I cried for my baby. The one with the angel wings. The one I would never hold in my own arms. I cried for the experiences that were now never going to happen. But I made sure that I cried once. This baby was never going to feel the jealousy or negativity of 'why not me.' This was no ones fault but Shane Amaro's. I shower this girl with love and affection.

"Anyway, this is your day, go and put the dress on."

I look over to my mom, whose eyes are glistening. She is almost back to her happy bubbly self. Dad got the best therapist in the world to work on her clock, and her clock only.

"I'll get it," my mom says, going to unhook it from where it is hanging on the door.

She brings it to me, placing it on my hands. "You look absolutely beautiful, Alaina." She makes no attempt to catch the tear that drops from her eye.

"Don't cry mama, or you will get me started." I take my dress, and drop my towel, revealing my underwear.

"Holy shit, Zane is going to eat you up in that," Vicky says.

I wiggle my eyebrows. "That's the plan," I say before putting on my strapless, pure white, wedding gown. It hugs me perfectly tight, before elegantly dropping around my feet; followed by a three-meter train. My hair hangs in a nicely put, loose, fishtail braid, which comes down over my left shoulder. Vicky added in little white roses through it as well, *she insisted*.

"Okay, I'm ready," I say, looking to my mom and Vicky.

Vicky is my only bridesmaid, wearing a soft, pale-pink, long, flowing dress. She picks up the flowers, before we make our way out to the waiting crowd on the beach.

We chose to get married at Zane's mother's house. Turns out, she owns a monstrous home that backs right on to the beach.

Steading my breaths, Vicky squeezes me. "Ready to hand your soul over?"

I laugh while taking my dad's arm. "He took it the day I first laid eyes on him."

I watch Vicky begin to walk down the Aisle, lined with white petals; as the orchestra and acoustic version of Metallica's *'Nothing Else Matters'* fills the air.

I start to make my way down the aisle, looking around nervously. I know the minute I lay my eyes on Zane, my whole world is going to stop.

Bringing my eyes up to the altar, I see him standing there, in a white long sleeve button up shirt, with his sleeves rolled up and his cut sitting proudly over his shirt. His hair is standing messy, but still tidy, as he smiles his earth-shattering smile at me.

I blush bright red while smiling back at him. I see Blake standing closest to him, followed by Ade, Felix, Harvey, Ollie and Chad. All dressed in the same clothes as Zane. At first I thought it would look ridiculous, me having one bridesmaid, while he has all five of his main men; but it doesn't, it looks perfectly, perfect.

When we reach him, my dad hands me over in the traditional way that fathers do. Zane slowly hooks his fingers into mine; pulling me into him as the minister begins to go through the traditional vowels. With a round of "I do's" Zane picks me up, and throws me over his shoulder. He slaps me straight on the ass, and then pumps his fist in the air in achievement. *Yeah that's right, you've finally legally laid claim on your women.*

THE END

Next by Author Amo Jones

Intricate Love
Sinful Souls MC Book Two

Blake and Vicky's Story

Vicky Abrahams has a tendency to get herself into tricky situations. But after a crazy spring break with one of her best friends, she has a bigger situation she needs to deal with—Blake Rendon.

Blake is part of the Sinful Souls MC. He has never been interested in anything serious with any woman, until Vicky. This interest results in him taking time to figure out his feelings for her.

Is it too late once he does?

Has Vicky already moved on?

Tired of all the secrets that almost broke her, she has every reason to be upset. But under it all, there's no one quite like Blake *fucking* Rendon.

Watch this story unravel as you meet new characters and new stories.

PLAYLIST

Metallica – "Nothing Else Matters" (Acoustic with Orchestra)
Disturbed – "Stricken"
Saving Abel – "Addicted"
Snoop Dogg – "Wiggle"

CONNECT *with me online*

Thank you for reading Perilous Love,
I hope you enjoyed reading it as much as I
enjoyed writing it.

Stay tuned for my new series "Westbeach" which
is coming soon, kicking off with Ryder and
Phoebe's story - "Losing Traction."

Thank you again to all my beautiful readers,
thank you for all your kind words and
encouragement.

You all inspire me to keep going—Thank you.

Goodreads

Add these books to your TBR list.
Perilous Love – Sinful Souls MC Series Book One
Intricate Love – Sinful Souls MC Series Book Two
Tainted Love – Sinful Souls MC Series Book Three
Losing Traction – Westbeach Series Book One

Website

http://www.amojonesauthor.com/

Twitter

https://twitter.com/authorAmojones

Email

amojonesauthor@yahoo.com

Facebook

https://www.facebook.com/amojonesauthor?ref=hl

Goodreads

https://www.goodreads.com/author/show/
14047384.Amo_Jones

Instagram

https://instagram.com/authoramojones/

ABOUT

the author
Amo Jones

A little bit about me. I am the mama bear to four little kiddos, two girls, and two boys. I'm also a wife-to-be to my partner of ten years. We were high school sweethearts, without the high school. My little (big) family are my rock, and I'm so lucky to have them with me through it all.

I am from New Zealand! Born and raised in a small town called Rotorua. It's a beautiful city, just smells a little. I'm currently living in Australia on the Whitsunday Coast (Great Barrier Reef) where we hope to settle down for a long time. I love the beach, and margaritas, and wine. Don't forget the wine. Chinese food is the best food.

One day I hope to travel the world, preferably the US, because I'm obsessed with it. I would travel now, but my bank account is like…"Dude, no." So I've put that in the goal bucket.

I love all my beautiful readers, you have kept me going. You're my inspiration to keep writing, with all your kind words and reviews. You are all amazing, and I write for you.

That's enough yappin' from me. See you all in Wonderland. x

Namaste.

Printed in Great Britain
by Amazon

46751796R00130